The Cowboy and His Obsession

Rock Springs, Texas Book 3

Kaci M. Rose

Five Little Roses Publishing

Blurbs

She's his best friend. He's the cowboy who's been obsessed with her for years.

Hunter has been my best friend since high school.

He fits in with my family, my brothers love him, my parents love him what more could I ask for.

At my brother's wedding seeing him in the arms of another girl ignites feelings I don't like.

When we sneak out of the wedding early something has changed.

The feelings I'm having have to stay hidden because I can't lose my best friend.

Megan has been mine since the day we met, she just doesn't realize it.

She's been chasing her dreams and I have been building a life for us.

She has no idea how obsessed with her I really am.

Seeing that little bit of jealousy in her is exactly what I needed to finally make my move.

But she's hell bent on staying friends, and I'm hell bent on making her, my wife.

It's a battle of wills and I'm a very patient guy. I've waited nin years for her.

What's a few more months?

Dedication

To the coffee that kept me going and the kids
that call me mommy.

Contents

Get Free Books!

Would you like some free cowboy books?
If you join Kaci M. Rose's Newsletter you get books free!
Join Kaci M. Rose's newsletter and get your free books!
Now on to the story!

Read the Audiobook!

This book is also available in audio! Get your copy to listen to as your read.
Get The Cowboy and His Obsession in Audio
https://www.kacirose.com/ObsessionAudio

Prologue

Megan

Eight Years Ago

I'm sitting on my friend Cindy's front porch waiting for her to get home from school. Honestly, she should have been here by now, but I'll give her the benefit of the doubt. Ever since we started our junior year of high school, she has been a bit boy crazy. This wouldn't be the first time I've been ditched after practice for a boy who caught her attention.

I'm sitting on her porch swing enjoying the nice breeze and thinking I'll give her twenty more minutes before I text my brothers and see who can give me a ride home. I know a few of them are still at practice. My sister Sage might even still be in town. Though I know she'd drop everything and come get me, no matter what.

I smile. I love my family. Blaze and Jason are my older brothers. The three of us are Mom and Dad's biological kids. Sage came along when Blaze found her parents abusing her. I don't know the details other than she, Blaze, and Colt are best friends, and Mom and Dad adopted Sage and then later, Colt after his parents died. Mac was adopted a few months ago. His parents were abusive too.

They've shielded me from the details and to be honest, I'm thankful for it, even if it makes me a bit of an outsider in the group.

The sound of a diesel truck catches my attention on the quiet street. Cindy lives in town, whereas my family lives on a large ranch about twenty minutes outside our small town of Rock Springs, Texas.

When I say small town, I mean the kind with one stoplight, and the cattle feed store is attached to the only café in town. There's one bar everyone ends up at on the weekends and if you want to know anybody's business, you just have to head down to the beauty salon for the latest gossip. I plan to own that beauty salon one day.

I watch as the most gorgeous guy I've ever seen gets out of the truck and walks up to the house across the street. He has blond hair and a large muscular frame. The way he walks, I just can't take my eyes off him.

I watch him walk up to the door, but no one answers after a few minutes. He walks back down to the sidewalk and looks down the street. When I can't help but laugh, the sound catches his attention, and he looks over at me. After a minute, he smiles then crosses the street.

"Hey," he calls from the sidewalk.

"Looks like we both got stood up." I stand up from the swing and walk down Cindy's steps.

He looks at the house behind me. I can tell he's trying to figure out who I'm waiting on.

"Your date ditch you?" I ask him, nodding to the house across the street I know one of the cheerleaders from school lives at.

"Looks like it. What about you?"

"My friend Cindy ditched me. A boy probably caught her attention. I was about to call my brother to give me a ride home." I approach the sidewalk where he's standing.

"What's your name?"

"Megan, what's yours?"

"Hunter."

"Nice to meet you, Hunter," I say and hold out my hand to shake his. He takes my hand,

and the jolt that goes through my hand takes over my whole body and shocks me.

I look up and meet his eyes. Blue. The most amazing blue eyes I've ever seen.

Danger, Will Robinson.

"What grade are you in?" he asks me.

"Junior, you?"

"Senior." He still hasn't let go of my hand, and it doesn't look like he has any intention of doing so.

"I'd be happy to give you a ride home seeing how my evening is suddenly free."

I laugh. "I live on a ranch outside of town."

"I don't mind."

"Okay, why not?" I shrug, and he walks me over to the passenger side of the truck. He opens the door for me and waits until I get in and buckle up before he closes it and gets in his side.

When he starts the truck, the local country station comes on to one of my favorite songs. I sing along, causing Hunter to laugh.

I give him directions to the ranch and keep singing. When the song ends, I have to ask him, "You really had a date with the cheerleader?"

He smirks. "A guy can hope, right?"

I shake my head. "Well, sorry it didn't work out."

He glances over at me. "I'm not."

I study him.

"Well, if you don't have other plans, why don't you stay and have dinner with us? Mom cooks for the ranch hands along with us, and there are always a ton of leftovers. Today, she's making her fried pork chops and biscuits. Colt sweet-talked her into it this morning."

He smiles again. "I'd really like that if you're sure it's okay."

"Promise. My mom will love having someone else to fuss over. Just be warned of my brothers and my sister. They're more protective than my parents."

He laughs. "Noted."

"So, what are your after high school plans? Everyone has been hounding me about it. It's all I can think of right now," I ask.

"I plan to become a vet like Dad. He owns the clinic here, and I'd like to join him on more house calls. I like going with him on those. What about you?"

"I want to buy the beauty shop in town. I love doing hair and makeup, but I don't want to leave the area. I love my family and the ranch, even if I don't want to work it every day like my brothers and sister do. I can take online classes, and I work part-time cleaning and answering phones there now."

"That's awesome that you already have a game plan set up."

"So do you."

Hunter fits right in with everyone at dinner. While my brothers give him the third degree, Sage just sits back and watches him. They ask what kind of grades he gets, and what he plans to do after school. My dad knows his dad, so they talk about the clinic a bit.

I know he wins my dad over when Dad offers to let Hunter work the cattle with him for Hell Week, the time we prep for winter and get the cattle checks done. We do it again in the spring too.

In the end, everyone seems to like him, and Mom invites him over anytime he wants.

I walk with him back to his truck later that night. It's the first time we're alone since the drive here.

"I really like your family." He smiles.

I smile. "They seem to like you too."

"What about you?" He studies my face.

"Jury is still out," I joke.

He runs his hand through his hair. "Well, let's fix that. Would you like to grab dinner tomorrow?"

I look him over. I don't like the way my body is reacting to him. I do like it, but I don't want it to act like this. He's supposed to be on a date with the cheerleader tonight, and now he's asking me out. I don't want to fall into that trap, but I'd really like to see him again too.

"I don't know. Maybe you can come over for dinner again tomorrow?"

He smiles. "I'd like that."

"Saturday, we're spending the day at the swimming hole on the ranch. You're welcome to join us."

"I'll be there. See you tomorrow at school, Megan."

Chapter 1

Megan

My brother Blaze is getting married today. He's the first to get married, though Sage and Colt are getting married in two months. I can't prove it, but I'm sure Mom and Dad adopted Colt just so Sage didn't lose him. I could tell from a young age, there was always something there, but now I've never seen them so happy.

I'm at the reception in the event barn on the ranch, watching Blaze and his new bride Riley on the dance floor, and they look so in love. I want that, but I can't let it get in the way of my dreams. I've been working at the beauty salon and once I finish school this semester, I finally get the last of the business signed over to me.

I've been working on it with Betsy the owner. She knows I want to own the shop, and she has no one to leave it to, so she has had me working there since I was sixteen, learning all aspects of the business. I started with cleaning and moved up to making appointments. Once I graduated high school, she has helped me get my license to do nails, then my makeup license, and finally the hair license.

After that, she has had me working a chair for a bit then has taught me the bookkeeping. She has made me an assistant manager of the shop and instead of a pay raise, she gave me 25% of the shop. She then started taking a few days off a week or coming in late, so she could help watch her grandkids.

The condition to get 25% more was to get my associate's degree in business management. I got another 25% when I took over the shop, and she retired to be with her family in Arizona. She'll give me the last 25% when I finish my bachelor's in business management. I have this last semester, and then it's all mine.

I can't let anything stand in my way of this. It's so close I can feel it. My family understands. Blaze and Riley are heading to the lake house for their honeymoon. We go as a family twice a year for a vacation. They invited us all out a week later to give Riley the full lake house family experience, but I declined. I need to finish this paper and some reading. So, a house to myself for a week is heaven.

I glance around the dance floor, trying to find Hunter. He's become my best friend, and one of my biggest supporters. He fits in great with my family and after that first dinner, he was always around. He's doing great in vet school and working with his dad at the clinic. He has been over helping with our cattle many times, so we give him a lot of hands-on experience. I can't believe after this semester, he only has one more year of school and he's a full-on veterinarian. I'm so proud of him.

Today, he's one of Blaze's groomsmen, and I'm one of Riley's bridesmaids, so we get to spend a lot of time together. I love spending time with him. I see him on the dance floor with Abby, Sage's friend who has been staying at the ranch. Her parents just died and having no other family, she's staying with us until she gets back on her feet.

Seeing Hunter with his arms around Abby, laughing on the dance floor, does something inside me. It can't be jealousy, right? Hunter is my best friend, but that's it. We're just friends. You don't get jealous of your friends. You want them to be happy. This is the first time

I've seen Hunter with another girl; that must be it.

Still seeing him with Abby has me unsettled. It's not that I don't like Abby. I do like her; she's such a sweet girl, and honestly, she'd be perfect for Hunter. So, why does that thought make me want to punch someone? I'm not a violent person, but I feel like I could be right now.

When the song ends, I walk over to Hunter and put on my best fake smile for Abby.

"Can I have the next dance?"

"Oh, of course. You two have fun," Abby says and walks over to Sage and Colt.

"You two seem to be having fun."

"Abby's a nice girl."

I look into his eyes and can't make out what the look in them is.

"Maybe you should ask her out," I say, even though it kills me to do so.

For a second, I think I see hurt flash across his face before it's gone, and I can't be sure.

"Abby's nice, but I'm not interested in her."

"You're interested in someone?" I ask, shocked I didn't know this.

I see a ghost of a smile cross his face. "Yeah, this girl has had my attention for a while now.

Won't give me the time of day though," he says and shrugs his shoulder.

"Who is it? Want me to talk to her?"

I get a full smile this time. "No, it's okay. Timing isn't good right now anyway."

We dance in silence for a bit, and I let it go. I don't think I want to know who has caught Hunter's interest. I've never seen him go on a date since we've been friends or even heard him talking about dating. We hang out all the time and until now, I've never given it a second thought.

I enjoy my dance with Hunter and try to ignore how it feels to have his hands on me. How my body tingles when his eyes are on me. How special I feel when I have his attention like nothing else around us matters.

He's always been there for me. When Riley's crazy ex-boyfriend showed up and the guys were worried about him breaking into the house, which he eventually did, Hunter let me stay at his place. He was my date to prom and every other dance at school after we met. Now, every time there's a business event in town or one for the ranch, we go together. I've gotten so used to it, and it's comfortable.

"You still not going to the lake house?" he asks.

"No, I need to finish this paper and get caught up on some reading."

"Care for some company? I told Sage I'd stay at the ranch while they were gone and watch the animals, but I can stay in a cabin if you don't."

"You're always welcome."

"Good. Plan at least one movie night; we haven't had one in a while."

I smile. I love our movie nights. They include popcorn, junk food, and Hunter makes some amazing milkshakes. We'll crash on the couch or the bed in my room and watch movies until we pass out.

"Deal."

Chapter 2

Hunter

This moment right here is one I want to commit to memory. Dancing with Megan in my arms, her body pressed up close to mine. I can almost pretend she's mine. What I wouldn't give for her to be mine.

I still remember the first day I met her. Seeing her walking down the steps of her friend's house, she was breathtaking. I'd never been so happy to be stood up on a date before. Dating a cheerleader was every guy's fantasy, but dating Megan is every guy's wet dream.

Megan is the girl next door—sweet and sassy, spunky, loyal, and beautiful. The natural kind of beauty that radiates from the inside out.

That day we met, I wanted nothing more than to call her mine. I tried many times to date her, but she kept putting me off, so I settled for friends. I know I affect her the way she does me. I see it. But we both have big dreams, and I know I can help her achieve hers by her side as her friend.

Now I want more, and I can't get her to give me a chance or see me as anything more than her best friend, a title I wear proudly. I wonder if she's scared to take that step or if she doesn't see me that way. I hate to push and lose the friendship, but the thought of seeing her with other guys doesn't sit well with me.

Megan means the world to me. I've been obsessed with her since day one. I know everything about her. Her favorite clothes, music, food. I know the face she makes when she's bored, and I can tell her fake smile from her real one. I know when she's lying to me, and I know before she does when she gets hungry or tired and needs a break.

After the song ends, I take a step back from her reluctantly.

"Want something to drink?" I ask her.

"Water please."

I nod and head over to the bar area and order two waters. Sage walks up beside me.

"So, any progress?" she asks. Sage has been my biggest supporter of Megan and me getting together. Somehow, she has noticed how I felt about her, so I guess I haven't been hiding it as well as I thought I have.

"No, she suggested I ask Abby out on a date. I had to tell her I wasn't interested in Abby."

I see disappointment cross her face.

"But she's letting me stay with her on the ranch while you guys are at the lake house."

"So, you need to step up your game and make your move."

"Yeah, here's to hoping an opportunity arises."

"Hey Hunter, didn't I hear your lease on your place is almost up?"

"Yeah, they're looking to sell it, so I need to find someplace else soon."

"Well, we have plenty of guest rooms, the one next to Megan's for one. You know we consider you family already. Just a thought."

I'm absolutely stunned speechless. Move into the ranch house and see Megan daily. Be in her space? Heck, in that room, I'd be sharing a bathroom with her.

"We can redecorate the room any way you like."

"You really want me there?"

Her face softens. "Hunter, ask anyone; you're family. I'm on your side here, and if Megan doesn't open her eyes soon, I'm going to take drastic measures. Anyone with eyes can see you two are meant to be. We'll help in any way we can."

I smile. "I think I'll take you up on that offer. But let's not say anything until after your trip. I want to see how the week plays out."

"Done."

I grab the waters and make my way back to Megan who's sitting at our table.

"So, we've been here a while, what do you think of sneaking out and taking the truck out for a bit under the stars?" I ask her.

She smiles at me then looks around. "Let's do it."

We hop in my truck and head to the west side of the ranch behind the main house where Megan, Sage, and her brothers live. I drive past the house a bit and pull over by one of the empty pastures. I leave the radio on low on the local country station, and I grab the blankets and pillows I keep in the backseat for just this reason and fix the bed of the truck up.

When I'm done, I look over at Megan in her bridesmaid dress, and my breath catches. Her long, brown hair is swept over her shoulder, and her makeup is natural and perfect. The dress fits her like a glove, hugging her curves. It's a pink lace that ends several inches above her knee. She has on her dressy cowgirl boots, and I've never seen her look more beautiful.

My heart races, and I don't think. "You look so beautiful, Megan," I whisper. I watch a flush cross her cheeks.

I lean in and place my hands on her waist and lift her up into the truck. I sit her on the tailgate, and I stand between her legs. I'm lost in her chocolate-brown eyes and when a piece of her hair falls forward into her face, I don't even think about it. I reach up and tuck it back behind her ear. Her lips part slightly, and I notice her breathing pick up.

She's just as affected by me as I am by her. Now I just need to get her to stop fighting it and admit it to herself. I rest my palm on the side of her face, and she closes her eyes and takes a deep breath. When she opens her eyes again, she looks right into mine. We just stand there and stare at each other. No words are said, but I feel like so much is said between us.

I clear my throat, breaking the spell. "Scoot on back, baby. Get comfortable."

I don't miss the shock on her face. I've never called her baby before that. A new line has been crossed, but she doesn't say anything. She just scoots back and lies down. I hop in and lie next to her. She scoots over and lays her head on my shoulder, and I wrap my arm around her.

We've done this many times before, and it's one of my favorites because I get to hold her. Here, we'll talk about anything and everything. It's like in the dark of night, it's easier to open up to each other, and I soak up any bit of her she's willing to give me.

"Have you started writing your paper at all?" I ask her.

"No, but I have my topic, and my outline is done. I also have a bunch of reading to do, and I'd like to get ahead in it. This is the last semester, Hunt. I'm so close I can feel it."

"I'm so damn proud of you, Megs. In a few more weeks, you'll own the shop. That's amazing."

"I know. I'm pretty excited."

"Will you let me plan something for your graduation? You and me a few days away?"

She doesn't answer right away.

"Yeah, I'd like that, Hunter. Thank you."

"Anything for you," I say. I've said this before, but I don't think she understands the meaning and intensity behind it. I would do anything for her, including stay friend zoned.

My mind races. I can't wait to dig into things to do. We stay out there for a few more hours, talking and staring up at the stars. I finally drop her back off at the main house just after midnight and head home, reminding myself I need to get some sleep and not stay up all night planning this trip.

Chapter 3

Megan

I've been sitting in front of my computer for a few hours now writing my paper, and I've reached a point where my mind is just blank. Everyone left yesterday for the lake house, and Hunter will be over later tonight. I have all day to write. I'm about halfway done but just stuck now.

I stretch and decide to go for a walk outside to clear my head a bit. I'll come back to do some reading. I change into jeans and a long-sleeve, blue-flannel shirt. It's at the weird point during the spring where it can get warm in the sunlight but be a bit chilly in the shade with a breeze. I put on my cowboy boots and head out.

I don't have any spot in mind. I just wander down behind the barn and into the cattle field by the house. This is where we keep the animals that are close to giving birth right now.

I walk back toward the tree line where I assume all the cattle is since I don't see them out here. On the way, Hunter crosses my mind. I feel like something changed at the wedding last week. I remember when he called me baby, sitting on his pickup truck. It had sent shivers down my spine in the best way.

Then the thought of going on a trip with him... Just he and I? I'm excited about that. Why does that excite me more than signing the paperwork and taking full ownership of the salon? This has been my dream for years; it's coming true, and I'd rather run off on vacation with Hunter.

Hunter.

He's texted me good morning every day since the wedding, and he's been here for dinner every night. He doesn't leave until I'm ready for bed. He's always finding ways to touch me and at least once a day, I catch him calling me baby.

I won't admit it, but I'm excited for him to come out tonight and spend the week here with me. I've always felt at peace around Hunter, no matter how crazy things get. One touch, and he can calm me right down.

I've made it to the tree line and decide to cut east to a clearing just before the creek. Hunter and I come out here a lot for picnics or just to talk. I feel like this is our spot. In the spring, it's filled with wildflowers that we always pick and bring back for the dining room table. Sage loves them and always asks us to get more while they last.

I'm excited about Sage's wedding in two months. If I'm honest, I'm excited to dance with Hunter again. She's having it at the ranch church on the other side of the property. It's the church our family built over a hundred years ago when there were no churches in the area. It's since stopped holding service with the church in town now, but we use it for weddings and funerals.

Riley had her wedding at the barn here on this side of the property since it's where she and Blaze first met. So, Sage's wedding will be the first in the church since Mom and Dad's wedding thirty years ago. We're all excited. Dad, Colt, and Blaze have been doing some repairs on the church. With a fresh coat of paint last summer, they're refinishing the hardwood floors and giving it a good cleaning.

It's going to be so pretty. I can't wait to see it. I've always dreamed of getting married there too. So, I'm excited to see it done up for a wedding.

I'm snapped out of my thoughts by a low groan. I know it's the type of groan cattle make when in labor. I hear it all the time on the ranch. As I near the clearing, I see a cow lying on the ground and make my way up to her. I check her tag number and recognize it as the one having twins. She isn't supposed to even be in her birth window for three more weeks.

She looks like she's having problems birthing, which is normal when a cow is having twins. I don't know what to do. Blaze and Sage normally handle these things and without thinking, I pull out my phone, thankful I have service, and call Hunter.

"Hey baby, taking a study break?" he answers in a soft voice.

"Hunter."

"Megan, what's wrong?" His voice is harsh and commanding. It's a tone you can't help but listen to.

"I went for a walk. I needed a break, and I found the cow who's having twins in the clearing we pick the wildflowers in. She's in labor, but she's struggling. Hunter, I don't know what to do."

"Megan, take a deep breath. I was just packing up to head your way. I'm walking out the door now. I'm going to text you a few things to get together for me and meet me at the barn, okay?"

"Okay, I'm heading back to the barn now."

"It's going to be okay, Megan."

"Just hurry."

I hang up and run back to the barn. When I get there, I pull up the text to see he wants things to put in the bed of the ranch truck and to pull it in the pasture. I do that then load up the truck. Blankets, a bale of hay, gloves, water, and soap. He also says to grab a shotgun and a box of shells since the blood can attract other animals out in the field like she is.

I run to the bunkhouse and Mike, get one of the ranch hands, to head to the barn and get a stall set up for us to bring the mom and babies back to later. I ask him to keep the ranch radio on him in case we need anything. It's more reliable than cell phones around the ranch.

I'm just coming out of the house with the shotgun when Hunter pulls up.

I run over to his truck, and he's barely out of the cab when he pulls me in his arms.

"You okay, Megs?"

"I am now that you're here."

"Good. I'm going to need your help."

I nod, and he grabs his bag and a box of stuff from his truck. We head to the ranch truck in the pasture behind the barn. He puts his stuff in the truck bed then walks me to the passenger door, lifts me into the seat, and buckles me in before running to his side.

"You said the clearing, right? Where we pick the wildflowers?"

"Yes." That's all I need to say. Hunter knows this land as well as I do.

We get as close as we can, and Hunter backs the truck up to the tree line before getting out. He grabs his bag and the water and has me grab the gun and the blankets. The walk to the clearing takes about a minute, and the cow is still in the same place as I left her.

"Don't rush her. You need to stay calm, otherwise she'll get upset. I need to examine her before we do much else."

We set our stuff down, and Hunter takes his bag with him.

"Stay by her head and speak in calm, shushing tones. Be ready to hold her down if needed."

"Okay." I know this part. I've helped Dad, Blaze, and Sage with many births over the years, just never twins. I know Blaze and Sage have been excited about this birth, so they've been talking about it some.

Hunter gets on the ground and opens his bag. He takes out a pair of gloves, removes his watch, and rolls up his sleeves. He puts the glove on that goes up to his shoulder and then looks at me.

"Ready?"

"Yes." I lean over the cow and try to be as calming as possible as Hunter sticks his hand in to examine her. You can tell when she feels him; she tries to jerk up, but I'm right there to hold her and calm her.

After a minute, Hunter pulls his arm out. "We have one breech and one facing the right way. The breach one is in front though. That's causing the problems."

"Ok, what do we need to do?"

"Megs, call Sage for me. I want to know the cow's history and get her permission to give her a light sedative."

I back up from the cow and pull out my phone to dial Sage.

"Hey Megs, how's the paper going?"

"Hey Sage, I went for a walk and found the cow that's having twins is in labor."

"Oh shit." I hear her call for Blaze in the background. "I'm putting you on speakerphone. Blaze and Colt are here too."

Hunter walks up and wraps a hand around my waist as I put her on speakerphone. "You're on speaker too. Hunter is here."

"Hey Sage, I just checked the cow. One calf is lined up right, and the other is breech. The breech one is upfront, causing some birthing problems. Is there anything I need to know about this animal?"

"No, she's been healthy. This is a natural twin conception. She wasn't slated to birth this round. I know twin births are a few weeks early, but not this early. She's still about three weeks early from her birth window."

"Can I get your permission to give her a light sedative since she's out in the field and use the calf puller if needed?"

"Oh Hunter, we trust you. You do what needs to be done." I feel his hand tighten on my waist for just a moment. I know what that simple statement means to him.

"Thank you, Sage."

"Call us later to let us know how it's going, okay?"

"Don't you worry. We got this," Hunter says.

"I don't doubt it. Later, Megs. Hunter, take care of her."

"I promise." He looks at me. We hang up, and Hunter walks back to his bag.

"With the sedative, she'll still be awake and know what's going on, but she won't jerk around like she was. She won't feel as much pain. I don't want to knock her out if we don't have to. If I do that, she's more likely to reject both calves."

I watch him measure liquid into a needle. Then he pushes the air from the needle and injects the liquid into the cow.

"Now we wait. Should be good in five to ten minutes. While we wait, let's spread out some hay to lay the calves in when they're born. I also need to grab the rest of the stuff from the truck. Stay here with her while I grab what I need, okay?"

I just nod while I watch the cow. I can't seem to take my eyes off her.

"Hey Megs." He walks over and wraps his arms around my waist. "We got this, I promise." With one hand under my chin, he brings my face to look at him. His eyes are soft, and I know he'll be a great vet. He knows what he's doing. He kisses the top of my forehead before heading down to the truck, and I'm left trying to catch my breath.

Hunter's back from the truck before I can catch my breath, and he has his work face on. I think we work well together. He's getting ready to pull the first calf out when he looks at me. He looks a bit worried which sets me on edge.

"What is it, Hunter?"

"Well, I really like that shirt on you. Soon as we get started, it's going to get ruined." I can't help but laugh as I stand and take it off. I have a black racerback tank top on under my shirt, and I toss the shirt off to the side. I swear I hear a sharp intake of breath from Hunter, but that can't be right.

Right?

He clears his throat and gives me directions. Within minutes, we have the first calf out, and he's carrying her to the first section of hay and lightly covering her. I stay with the first calf and watch him work to birth the second.

Watching him work and doing what he loves is a sight to be seen; he's in his element. Watching his muscles ripple and the look of concentration on his face is sexy as hell.

Wait, did I just say that?

I can't think Hunter is sexy; he's my best friend. You don't think your best friend is sexy.

I watch him some more, and there just isn't another word for him. I remember back to the day we met, and I remember thinking he was the best-looking guy I had ever seen. That was teenager Hunter. Hunter as a man now is panty melting.

He could have any girl he wants, yet he doesn't date. He spends his free time with me, and I don't think I've appreciated that. I need to make sure he knows I enjoy having him around.

When he has the second calf in his arms and sees that she's okay, the largest smile lights up his face. When his eyes lock on mine, my whole body warms. Have I always had this crush on Hunter? What does this mean for our friendship?

Danger, Will Robinson. Danger.

Don't you dare let this affect the best friendship you have, Megan.

Don't. You. Dare.

He lays the second calf down then goes back to check on the mom. Once the placenta is delivered, the mom takes a bit to get on her feet but when she does, she walks over to sniff the calves.

Hunter walks up to me and pulls me away from the calves to let their mom do her thing. I feel my back hit his solid chest, and he wraps his arms around my waist. He leans his face down to my ear.

"Now we wait to make sure she accepts them both and feeds before we take them back to the barn."

He doesn't move. We just stay there and comfort each other. We watch the mom clean off one calf then walk over and sniff the other. She walks around the second one and cleans her as well.

I smile as I feel Hunter bury his head in my neck.

"You did it," I whisper.

"No, we did it," he says into my neck then kisses me just below my ear, causing my body to shiver.

"Hunter..." I whisper, not sure if I'm warning him to stop or begging him to continue. He leaves his head buried in my hair for a minute more before lifting it and taking a deep breath. He doesn't move other than that, and we stand to watch the mom with her babies.

Here in his arms feels right, like this is where I'm supposed to be, but Hunter isn't mine, and this can't be where I'm supposed to be.

As the calves try to stand, Hunter reminds me to call Sage and let them know how it went while he cleans up.

He takes everything back to the truck while I talk to Blaze and Sage and watch the mom with her new babies. She has accepted both, but Blaze reminds me that they both still need a bottle of the cow drink tonight, then twice a day until they get home. He tells me that the ranch hands can do it and which ones to talk to. They also ask me to send pictures.

When I get off the phone, Hunter is back, and Mike is behind Hunter with what looks like a rope in his hand. I notice Hunter has a shovel in his hand.

"We need to bury the hay the calves were on and the placenta, so we don't draw in other animals looking to feed. Then we'll carry the calves to the truck. The mom should follow but just in case, we have the rope." Hunter gets busy digging a hole to bury everything as the calves walk around a bit more.

I take some photos for Sage and Blaze and can't help noticing how darn cute these babies are. I take way more photos than necessary. I even manage to sneak a few of Hunter with his muscles rippling as he digs the hole. How could I not?

Once ready, Hunter and Mike pick up a calf and slowly make their way to the truck. I follow, making sure the momma cow follows. Once back to the barn, Mike mixes us up some of the calf drink in the bottles before heading out. Hunter wants to stay and watch the calves for a bit longer.

"Well, let's get this in them, so we can let them get settled for the night. Mike said he was sending a guy out here on barn patrol. They will take shifts for the next few nights." He hands me a bottle.

We head into the stall and sit with our backs to the sidewall and pull a calf into us as they drink from the bottle. They seem to like the drink because we have no problems getting them to drink it.

Chapter 4

Hunter

Watching Megan feed the calf is one of the sexiest things I've seen. She has the passion for the beauty salon and loves to get all dolled up but isn't afraid to get her hands dirty and help at the ranch too. It's one of the many things I love about her.

Her eyes catch mine, and the heat I see in them makes me breathless. She is slowly taking me all in and having her eyes on me makes my skin tingle and my cock twitch. I have to turn my eyes back to the calf in front of me; this isn't a good time to pop wood.

I get myself under control and glance over at Megan again, but she's looking at my lips while licking hers. I can't stop the groan I let out. Her eyes flick to mine, and a light blush creeps up her face, making her look even sexier.

As the calves finish up their bottles, we stand and head out of the stall. I take Megan's empty bottle and head off to clean them. I can't get the sight of Megan feeding that calf just now out of my head. Sitting against the side of the stall in her jeans and her black tank top with her hair pulled up in a messy bun, and no makeup on, she looked amazing, and I've never seen a sexier sight.

I give myself a minute to commit that image to memory before I push it aside and try to get my cock under control again. I take a few deep breaths and reach down to readjust myself before heading back to Megan.

When I come back, I see Megan leaning against the gate with her hands on the rail, watching the mom with the calves. I walk up behind her and hoping since she didn't push me away in the field, that she won't now.

I press my front to her back and place one hand on the gate and one arm around her waist. I feel her body melt into mine, and I know she can feel how hard I am against her ass, but she doesn't seem to care.

"What's on your mind, baby?" I ask.

"You are actually." I'm a little startled by that answer. I love that I'm on her mind, but that was the last thing I expected her to say.

"What about me?"

"How different you seem. How much I enjoyed watching you work today. You're amazing at what you do, Hunter."

I smile. "Thanks, Megan. I enjoyed having you by my side today."

She looks over her shoulder at me again. Then her eyes drift down to my lips, and her tongue comes out again, licking hers. I can't take it anymore; I have to take my chance. I send up a silent prayer that I'm not about to mess everything up.

I lean in so slowly, letting her know my intention and giving her time to stop me. When she doesn't, I touch my lips to hers, and the little gasp that comes from her makes me rock hard. The whole barn fades away as she melts into me and kisses me back.

I bring my hand to the back of her head and hold her closer to me as I deepen the kiss. I run my tongue along the seam of her lips and when she opens for me, I let my tongue tangle with hers. This moment is better than any kiss I could ever dream of with her. She feels so much better than I ever could have dreamed of.

She slowly turns from the gate, wraps her arms around my neck, and pulls me in closer, melding her body to mine and letting out a small moan. I press her back to the gate and fight not to grind against her. I focus on her mouth and how amazing she tastes. Like summer and that cherry Chapstick she's always wearing.

After a few moments, I pull back to catch my breath and look at her. Her eyes are still closed but when she opens them, she's a bit dazed. Knowing I've given her that look makes me want to bang on my chest caveman style.

I rest my forehead on hers and smile. That moment is everything I've always dreamed it would be and so much more. My first kiss with Megan. The first of many, I hope.

After a minute, when she catches her breath, she says, "Hunter..." I can hear the protest in her voice and not wanting to ruin this moment, I grab her hand.

"Let's head inside and get some dinner. We can talk then."

Once inside, I head to the fridge and pull out some of Sage's leftovers and warm them up for us. I pour two glasses of sweet tea and take them to the table. As I head back to the kitchen for the plates, I can't help the smile on my face. I love taking care of her and if she'll just let me, I'd take the best care of her for the rest of my life.

Once we sit to eat, I can feel her eyes on me before she talks, "That kiss was amazing, Hunter."

I look up at her and can't stop the smile that spreads across my face if I try. "Yeah, it was."

"But we can't do this," she says, and my heart sinks.

"Why not?"

"You're my best friend and the thought of losing you if this doesn't work out? It will kill me. Plus, I only have a few weeks left of school. I can't get distracted."

I don't reply right away and mull over her words in my head. I had planned to wait until she graduated. I know how important school is to her. I also know she'd use it as an excuse to push me away. She graduates in less than three weeks. We both have finals coming up.

I don't want to start anything big, but I just couldn't stop myself today. The moment was perfect, and I wouldn't change it for the world.

"So, we take it slow, Megs."

"Hunter..."

"I heard you, I promise. But we're adults. We can make a promise right here and now that we don't let this affect our friendship. We promise that if it doesn't work out, we take a breath no more than a few days, and we put it behind us and go right back to being friends. In fact, let's say four days later, we have a mandatory movie marathon, and you can pick the movies."

I know that will catch her attention, getting full movie control. We fight over that all the time. I think she gets a kick out of making me watch chick flicks with her, but I don't think she understands. I'd watch anything just to spend time with her. I think me sitting through *Magic Mike* proved that.

She looks down at her plate and doesn't look me in the eye when she says, "I don't want to start anything until I'm done with school."

Holy shit, that's not a no. I have to stop my jaw from hitting the ground.

"Okay, so we just keep being friends and let things go at their own pace. We can talk after graduation. But Megan?" I wait for her to look at me. When she does, I say, "I'm not going anywhere. I'll wait until you're ready. I've waited all this time already, what's a few more weeks?"

I see a bit of shock on her face, so I know it's time to change the subject.

"Tomorrow, I have to head out to the rodeo and do some animal checks. I have to head back tomorrow night. Want to go with me? We get good seats, and I'm just there in case one of the animals gets hurt."

I see her smile. "We go every year, so yes, I'd like to go, but I need to get some reading done beforehand that I didn't get done today."

"I promise to wake you up before I leave and let you read in peace tomorrow."

After dinner, we head to the living room to watch some TV and unwind. I sit on the couch and pull up Netflix. Megan sits next to me and curls up to my side. I'm a bit shocked, but I roll with it and wrap my arm around her. I put on the new action movie we've been talking about and settle in.

About twenty minutes into the movie, I hear Megan's breathing even out. I look down and sure enough, she's asleep. Wanting to enjoy the time with her in my arms like this, I finish the movie. I debate shifting and lying with her on the couch, but I want her to be comfortable. After watching her sleep for another ten minutes, I carefully pick her up and carry her to her room.

Chapter 5

Megan

I have the most amazing staff at the beauty shop. I've been able to take several days off to study, and there have been no issues. I just check in and make sure everything is running smoothly.

I spend the morning catching up on reading and even get a bit more of my paper written. Hunter left early this morning to head out to the rodeo, but he woke me with a kiss and told me he left me breakfast downstairs, his famous cinnamon-honey French toast.

I was up and downstairs eating before he was out the door. True to his promise, he doesn't even text so I can study.

Now I'm getting ready for the night, and I can't help but feel like this is a date. A casual date since he's there working but still a date. I stand in the middle of my room thinking about what to wear. When Sage had the house redone, we each redecorated our bedrooms. I chose what many would call a farmhouse décor, and I still love it. It's like something out of a magazine and normally, it helps calm me.

I have hardwood floors and light-gray walls with white wood accents and blue all over. There's a sitting area in front of the windows and a desk in one corner and of course, a makeup vanity. A barn door leads to the bathroom and another to the closet.

I love my room, and it's always been my getaway. It feels a bit empty right now, and I can't put my finger on it. I head into my closet to plan my outfit for tonight. Hunter did say it would be an unseasonably warm night tonight.

I grab a pair of black shorts and put on a white tank top and look for a shirt to wear. I settle on a blue plaid shirt with a hint of red. I roll the sleeves up and leave the first few buttons undone to show some cleavage. I pair it with my cowboy boots.

I decide to leave my hair down but put some curls in it since I'll have my cowboy hat, and I apply some light makeup. I decide to skip bringing a bag and put my ID, debit card, and a bit of cash in my bra. I'm just checking over my appearance when there's a knock on my door.

I take a deep breath and answer it to see Hunter, and he takes my breath away. He looks freshly showered in jeans that fit him well and a gray plaid shirt. When my eyes land back on his face, I see he's still taking me in.

"Megs," he says breathlessly and then clears his throat. "You look beautiful, baby."

I smile. "You look pretty damn good yourself." I watch a smile cross his face.

"You ready?" He holds out his hand.

He walks me down to his truck and helps me inside. On the way to the rodeo, he talks about his day and the animals he saw. He asks about my reading and how the paper is coming. We talk a bit about the new calves as well.

The rodeo is already abuzz with life even though we're early. Hunter parks in the back and comes to open my door. He takes my hand as we walk in.

"You hungry? Food is set up and lines will be short now."

"I love rodeo food. Let's dig in."

A chili corn dog, taco nachos, and a cheesecake on a stick later, we head toward the back of the rodeo as everything gears up. As we walk, I notice women checking out Hunter left and right. It doesn't seem to matter that he's holding my hand. I just shake my head.

"What's wrong, baby?"

I laugh. "It's nothing."

He squeezes my hand. "Come on, tell me."

"The women here aren't even trying to hide the fact that they're checking you out, even though you're holding my hand."

He laughs. "I was just thinking the same thing about you, baby."

"What? I haven't seen one guy check me out."

"Because you've been focused on the girls checking me out. Same with me, I haven't seen the girls because I've been focused on the guys checking you out."

I sigh and shake my head. "Okay, I'll stop. Let's have some fun."

We walk around the back, checking things out. Hunter shows me the different holding pens, talking about the different animals when the rodeo starts. The energy back here is infectious, and I can't help but get even more excited.

Along one metal fence, a row of cowboys are sitting on top of it all in their wranglers, plaid shirts, cowboy hats, and cowboy boots.

Off to the side from there in clear view are all the buckle bunnies, whispering and giggling.

Hunter shakes his head. "Let's not go that way," he says, and I agree.

We get front row seats down on the right side, so Hunter can hop to the back if needed. The feel from the front row is electrifying. You can feel the pounding of hoofs on the ground and see full force when a man or animal hits the ground. I cringe several times. These rodeo cowboys are no joke.

I love watching the trick horse riders. I know Sage has trained several horses for this before, and I've seen her do a few tricks but nothing like we see here at the rodeo tonight. After that, they bring the kids who are roping sheep and baby cows. They're adorable and damn good for their ages.

During the intermission before the bull riding, which is the main event, Hunter takes me to the back again to check on the animals that were just out, even though there doesn't seem to be any visible injuries.

He's listening to a horse's heart rate when a group of girls walks by, and I hear them. It's like they aren't even trying to hide it.

"Damn, with a vet like him, I think I need to adopt a dog," girl one says.

"If I'd have known he was the vet, I wouldn't have made Dad get rid of that ugly dog hanging around the house," girl two says while licking her lips.

Then an eruption of giggles startles the horse. I see something I don't think I've ever seen from Hunter. Pure anger.

He flips around to the girls. "Do me a favor and don't ever get a pet. They deserve better treatment than that. Since you don't have a reason to be back here, it's time to return to your seats. You're now upsetting the animals. And for the record, girls like you are why I work ranches and not the clinic."

Then he turns to me and places a hand on my cheek. "Ready to get back to our seats, baby?" All I can do is nod. I'm totally speechless.

I see the girls' jaws drop, a few of them blush. At least they have the decency to be embarrassed, but when the leader looks to start to say something, Hunter beats her to it.

"Hey Jimmy!" he calls out. A moment later, a bulked-up security guard shows up. "Please show these ladies back to their seats. They're disturbing the animals."

"Sure thing, Hunter," he says and turns to the girls. The leader has the nerve to stomp her foot like a five-year-old who hasn't gotten her way. I'm guessing she doesn't get told no very often.

Once they head out, Hunter packs up his things, and I still haven't said a word. I see a bit of unease in Hunter's eyes as he watches me. Before I can think better, I take his hand.

"Come here," I say and pull him out back to the parking area between the trailers.

I push him up against the wall of one of the trailers and before I can think better of it, I kiss him. After a few seconds of shock, he kisses me back. With one arm around my waist and one hand in my hair, he flips me around, so I'm the one pressed against the side of the trailer and kisses me like he's been at war, and this is the first time he's seen me in years.

I guess this is the first time I've kissed him. In this moment, I don't know why I'm not kissing him more. This kiss is hot and intense. I feel him press into me and feel his hard erection against my belly. His tongue makes love to mine in a way that I wish it's another part of him.

It all feels so good, making me groan. He pulls back and rests his forehead on mine as we catch our breath.

"Why did you stop?" I ask.

"Because no one gets to hear those sexy moans but me. As much as I love kissing you, I don't want anyone to see you like this either."

He runs his hands down the sides of my face, smiling at me. Then all sense crashes back to me, and I rest my head against his chest.

What did I do? Why did I kiss Hunter? God, that kiss though. But this could ruin everything.

"I can hear those wheels turning. That kiss was hot, Megs, and we can still take this slow. I'm not pushing for anything, and I'm not going anywhere."

"Okay." We stand there for a few minutes, arms wrapped around each other before he pulls back.

"We better get back to our seats." He takes my hand.

As we slowly walk back, I have to ask, "Is that why you took on working the ranches versus the clinic?"

He gives me a half-smile. "Yeah, I got tired of the girls coming in to flirt with me, so I talked to Dad. He was ready to slow down, so we switched. I took the ranch work, and he now stays at the clinic, calling me in only when he needs help, or if there's a case he wants me to see."

I nod. "But having them come into the clinic like that, I'm sure makes it easier to get dates."

I watch anger cross his face. "You think girls like that are what I want, Megan? I know you've had me friend-zoned for years, but I never wanted to be there." He stops and takes a deep breath as I try to figure out what he means.

"I want to make this perfectly clear to you. I haven't been on a date since I met you. Have you asked yourself why?"

My mind races. It never occurred to me to question why he never dates or talks about dating. Heck, he doesn't even talk about other girls, ever. What time does he have to spend with other girls? He's working or with me and my family or with his family.

He's always been with me. Talking to me. Then that kiss. *That kiss.*

I'm almost too scared to hope. "Why?" I whisper.

"Because you're the only one I want. I've wanted you from the day I was standing on the sidewalk watching you come down those steps of Cindy's house. I've wanted you since the first night at dinner with your parents. No other woman even catches my eye. I've been okay being friend-zoned because I get to stay close to you, but I'm not holding back anymore, Megs."

He takes a step closer and lifts my chin, so I'm looking into his eyes.

"I promised you we can go slow, and we will. Once you graduate, all bets are off. Do you understand me?"

I nod, and he leans down to give me a chaste kiss on the lips before backing up and taking my hand again.

"Now, let's enjoy the rest of the rodeo."

We get back to our seats and remain standing to watch the bull riding. Hunter puts his arms around my waist, bringing my back to his chest. That's how we remain for the rest of the rodeo. It doesn't escape me then I've never felt safer than I do now with thousand-pound bulls bucking and spinning less than a hundred feet away from me.

Chapter 6

Hunter

It's been a week since our rodeo date and like I promised, we're taking it slow. I've slipped back into best-friend mode, so I don't push her too far too fast, even if all I want is her in my bed every night. Every morning, I've been texting her to let her know she's on my mind, telling her I hope she has a good day.

I text her throughout the day—photos of the animals I'm working with and funny things that happen—and she does the same. Then every night, I'm out at the ranch with her for dinner.

What she doesn't know is things are about to change. Her brothers will be here any minute to help me move my stuff to the ranch. Sage has suggested I don't say anything and just let it happen. She promises to take the heat if it backfires.

I hear the doorbell and answer the door.

"Hey man, you packed and ready?" Blaze says.

"Yeah, I have a few things going to storage and a few people coming by to buy some furniture. The rest is ready to go."

"Okay, point and tell us what to do," Colt says as he steps into my apartment, followed by Jason and Mac. I can't help but smile. They never give it a second thought. Sage had said I needed help to move my stuff, and they had just asked when. They all brought their trucks, and here they are.

"Let's start with this stuff. It's going to the storage center across town." I point to the stuff to the side of my living room. We get it loaded in two trucks. I then give the guys instructions on what to load up while we run to the storage unit.

By the time we get back, they have almost all the boxes loaded. Over the next few hours, we move a bit slower as people come in to buy some of the furniture—the couch, the dining room table, a dresser, and my TV.

The guy buying the TV makes a joke about how sad I must be to have to sell it, but I'm not. Yeah, it's a nice TV, but I'd give up TV all together just to have my Megan. I don't see giving up my TV and my apartment as a sacrifice; I'm gaining so much more.

I tell him this, and he just shakes his head. Once he leaves, the guys all stand shoulder to shoulder with their arms crossed, looking at me. If I hadn't grown up with these guys, it would be very intimidating.

"What?" I ask.

"You feel that way about our sister?" Blaze asks with no emotion on his face.

"I do. I've wanted her from the first time she brought me home for dinner. I tried more times than I can count to get her to go on a date with me then decided to be her friend and let her go through school. In that time, I have fallen in love with her. She graduates in just over a week, and I'm not holding back after that."

I figure they deserve the truth to lay it all out on the line. Their faces give away nothing, so I just wait for one of them to speak next.

"You treat her right. I know Sage is in on all this and is rooting for you, but we won't hesitate to kick your ass," Colt says.

I smile. "Good, I wouldn't have it any other way."

We finish loading up and head out to the ranch. We mostly carry boxes up to my room, next door to Megan, which means we'll be sharing a bathroom. I know this will piss her off. She likes not sharing her bathroom but since it's attached to my room too she will be.

We've moved just over half the boxes into my room when Megan's truck pulls up.

"What's all this?" she asks.

"Your boy here is moving in," Mac says with a smile on his face.

"What?!" Megan asks, her head snapping back to look at me.

"Well, my lease was up, and the owners are looking to sell, so they aren't renewing any leases. Sage offered me to stay here at the ranch for the time being, and I took her up on it, especially with the summer coming up and all."

I watch her purse her lips, which I know means she's mad but thinking. Then she sighs.

"What room are you moving into?" she asks.

Jason laughs. Asshole.

"The room next to yours," Blaze says.

"You aren't sharing my bathroom!" she screeches in the most adorable way.

I can't help but smile and walk over to her. I place one hand on her waist and lean in.

"I am, baby, and soon I'll be sharing your bed too," I whisper in her ear and walk off to grab another box, leaving her speechless.

Once up in my room, I unpack my clothes. A few minutes later, Megan walks in but doesn't move past the doorway.

"You really are moving in. Why didn't you tell me?"

"Sage's idea. You'll have to ask her." She narrows her eyes on me. It's a cop out, and we both know it, but she lets it slide.

She walks in and flops down on my bed.

"Fine, but you better not leave the seat up. You better flush the toilet and don't use my sink and clean up after yourself."

"Come on, this isn't the first time we've shared a bathroom. I wasn't that bad, was I?"

She just looks over at me but doesn't answer.

"Hey, so you have tomorrow off, right?" I ask, trying to switch gears.

"Yes."

I smile. "Want to go mudding?"

This girl loves doing her hair and makeup, you would never know it, but she also loves to head down to the mud spot on the ranch and get dirty. It's supposed to rain tonight, so it'll be the perfect time to go.

A smile crosses her lips. "Yeah, we haven't been in a while." She gets up and helps me finish unpacking.

"Next time just tell me. I don't like being kept in the dark, and I would have wanted to help," she says so softly, almost like she's hurt.

Fuck. The last thing I want is to hurt her.

I walk over to her and pull her in my arms. "I promise, baby. From now on, we talk about everything. It's you and me. I should have told you, and I'm sorry. I was just worried you'd say no, and I wanted this so bad. I want to be near you."

She nods, and we stand in each other's arms as I soak her in for another minute before we get back to unpacking.

That night, I'm woken up by someone crawling into bed with me. I look over and see a sleepy Megan sliding in next to me. I wrap my arm around her and pull her close to me.

"Can't sleep?" I ask.

"Not with you being so close by. Think this will backfire on us?"

I lean down and kiss the top of her head. "Not if we don't let it."

She's quiet for so long I think she might have fallen back asleep, but she tilts her head up to look at me.

"I like you being here."

I smile, and the five little words warm my heart. "I like being here too."

She shocks me again and leans up and kisses me. It's light and teasing but when I kiss her back, she deepens the kiss.

As much as I want to flip her over and kiss all of her, I know she said slow, so I let her lead the show even if every nerve in me is on fire and my cock is harder than rocks right now.

She slowly turns to get a better angle, never breaking the kiss. I bring my hand up to tangle in her hair, needing the connection and wanting to pull her closer all at once. When I feel her straddle me and my cock resting against her heat, I groan.

"Megan..." I whisper, "This why you couldn't sleep, baby?"

"Yes." There's enough light to see her nod and the slight blush on her face.

"I'll take care of you, baby."

I can't help but smile against her lips. She runs her hands down my chest and under my shirt. Then she tries to pull my pants down. I reach down and grab her hands.

"Not like this, Megs," I whisper.

"Hunter?"

I look into her eyes. "I want you. Don't get me wrong." I thrust my hips up so she can feel me. "I want you very much. But I've waited all this time for you, and I don't want our first time to be here like this. I want it to be perfect and not have to worry about one of your brothers walking in."

She grinds against me, now letting out a small gasp.

"Are you saying that you haven't..."

I smile and take a deep breath. "I'm a virgin, just like you, baby. I have saved myself for you, and our first time won't be rushed or someplace we have to keep quiet, okay?"

She nods.

"But if you can promise to be quiet, I'll take care of you tonight. Can you be quiet, baby?"

"Yes," she whispers again.

I grab her hips and slowly grind her against me.

I may be a virgin, but I've done my research. I want her first time to be amazing. I have heard the guys and girls talking in school about how their first times were short and sucked. I don't want that for us. She deserves to have an amazing first time and to be cherished. That is what I plan to give her.

I know how to please her. How to make her come and how to make it as pain-free as possible, in theory.

"I can't wait to learn your body baby, learn what you like, and what makes you come."

"Hunter," she moans.

"I got you, baby," I say and thrust up as I grind against her. She sits up and tosses her head back then, thrusting her chest out. I notice her thin tank top. She isn't wearing a bra. Her nipples are hard, stiff peaks telling me just how turned on she is.

I lean up to take one into my mouth over her shirt and bite ever so lightly, causing her hips to jerk.

"Quiet, baby. I don't want anyone to come in here and see you like this. Only me."

"Only you," she whispers, staring into my eyes.

I slow my thrusting down.

"Tell me you're mine, Megan. I need you to be mine."

I see her hesitate.

"We can still go slow. You set the pace until you graduate, but I need you to be mine. Only mine."

"I've been yours from day one. I was scared to admit it."

That confession steals my breath, and I double my efforts, grinding her on my cock. With one change in angle, she comes. When a small moan escapes, I pull her mouth down to mine and swallow the rest of her moans.

Megan coming apart for me is the sexiest thing I've ever seen. Another thrust and I'm coming in my pants. The feeling is so good, I don't even care.

She lies on my chest, catching her breath as I catch mine. Finally, I roll her to the side.

"I need to clean up. Stay here, okay?" I watch her nod.

I quickly clean up and change my boxer briefs and pants, then crawl back into bed with her.

Falling asleep with her in my arms results in the best sleep I've ever had. She has a calming effect on me, and the last thought I have before drifting off is I hope I can spend the rest of my life falling asleep with her in my arms just like this.

Chapter 7

Megan

I wake up and can't help but smile. I haven't even opened my eyes, but I'm happier than I've been in a long time. I stretch, and that's when I feel another body next to me. I freeze. Everything rushes back to me from last night.

Hunter.

I slowly open my eyes to look over at him, only to find him resting on one arm, looking down at me.

"Good morning, beautiful," he says softly.

I can't help but blush; I'm sure I look a mess.

"That was the best night and the best sleep of my life," he whispers then leans in to lightly kiss my neck. My nipples harden, and I can't stop the moan. It feels so good.

I feel him smile against my neck, but he says nothing, just wraps his arm around my stomach.

"Ready to go mudding? It rained last night, so it will be a blast." He pulls away to look me in the eye.

I'm trying to process how I feel about last night and waking up in Hunter's bed. His bed, that's right next door to mine now.

I wait for the panic over the thought of losing my best friend, but it doesn't come. This all feels right. I want this, but the thought of losing him is still in the back of my head. I don't think I could survive losing him, but I want to see where this goes.

I couldn't believe it last night when he admitted to being a virgin too. I guess it makes sense being he hasn't dated and all, but I never thought about it. It may be weird, but I think that's what calms me. He's as inexperienced at all this as I am.

I take a deep breath. "Let's go mudding."

We get up and get ready, fighting over bathroom usage just like we always would. Nothing seems to have changed, and it's a relief.

While I grab breakfast for us, he loads up the four-wheeler on the trailer, and we head out, eating in his truck on the way. It's been a while since we've been mudding. It's always been a fun way for us to relax and de-stress together.

The rainstorm last night brought in some cooler weather today, so I'm in jeans and a sweatshirt. Hunter is in jeans and a long-sleeve gray and black raglan shirt, one of my favorite styles on him. He catches me looking at him and smiles.

"What?" he asks.

I shake my head. "I'm just liking this, is all."

He smiles back and reaches out to grab my hand. "Me too."

We get down to the mud hole, and Hunter gets the four-wheeler off the trailer while I check out the mud hole. It looks like it'll be a lot of fun today.

"Ready?" Hunter calls.

I grab two baseball caps out of his truck, not that it will be much help saving our hair, but it's a small tradition we've always done.

Hunter drives first, so I hop on behind him and hold on tight. I think Hunter is a little more careful when I ride with him; he worries about me, but we still have a blast. He's good at hitting a puddle just right to make it spray everywhere.

After about ten minutes, another truck pulls up, and out comes Blaze and Riley. We stop to greet them.

"Hey guys," Blaze calls, "Looks like we had the same idea."

"Come on in. It's perfect today!" I call back.

"Would you believe Riley has never been mudding?" Blaze calls back, talking about his new wife. I can see the love in their eyes when they look at each other, and I can't help but smile. "We're here to take it easy, precious cargo and all."

Blaze rubs Riley's stomach as they stare at each other. They announced at their wedding reception that they're expecting, and the family is so excited.

"Well, you should call Sage and Colt, give her the full experience," I say.

"They're already on their way," Riley says just as Colt's truck appears around the corner.

They unload their four-wheeler while Blaze and Hunter talk for a minute.

"Hold on!" Hunter calls back to me, and I laugh as he circles the pit again, spraying mud across the four of them, making Riley squeal. Sage and the guys laugh.

I'm laughing so hard, I bury my head into Hunter's back to prevent mud from getting in my mouth. We have all learned the hard way;

while the mud is good to play in, it kind of sucks in the taste department.

Sage and Colt join us in the mud, and it looks like Blaze and Riley are watching for a bit. We can't have that.

I lean over to Hunter's ear. "Spray 'em!" I watch a huge smile cross his face. On the next pass, he gets Blaze and Riley good, but I have to give points to Blaze for stepping in front of Riley and taking the brunt of it.

Moments later, they're on their four-wheeler and joining us in the pit. They are running circles much slower than the rest of us but still spraying up mud, yelling and laughing, and having a good old time. When we all finally stop to take a break, we're covered in mud.

I hop down and head over to Riley.

"What do you think?"

"OMG, I've never had so much fun getting so dirty!"

"That's what she said!" Sage yells, and we all bust out laughing while a light flush coats Riley's cheeks.

"You ready to drive? It's the girls' turn now!" I say.

She has a huge smile on her face. "Let's do this!"

I walk back over to Hunter, and he has a huge smile on his face too. "Ready?"

"Always," he says as I climb in front of him. He wraps his arms around me and scoots so his front is pressed against my back, which instantly scrambles my brain. Sage and Colt head out first as I take a deep breath and try to unscramble my thoughts.

"You okay, Megs?" Hunter leans in and whispers against my ear. His hot breath doesn't help matters much but when a spray of cold mud hits us, it's all I need to snap back into action.

"Let's do this!" I say as I take off and chase after Sage with Riley behind us taking it a bit slower. Sage gains some speed then starts doing donuts, sending mud flying everywhere. I get a few good spins in, hitting Sage and Colt before Riley seems to loosen up and get a few on us as well.

By the time, we stop again. We're all smiling and laughing. I jump off and head over to Riley and hug her.

"So, still having fun?"

"Are you kidding? I love it! I can't believe I haven't tried it before now!"

"Good, it's a great way to de-stress around here."

I hear Sage and Colt arguing, so I turn to face them.

"You aren't tracking that mud up to the bathroom, Colt!"

"But the rain shower will clean me off better."

"Just no! We all shower at the barn. It's why we leave a set of clothes there. Once you're clean, you can use the shower."

"She's right, you know!" I yell. "Always been. We clean up at the barn. No mud in the house; she and I have to clean it!"

"Me too now!" Riley interjects and smiles at me.

The men all laugh, and I see Hunter watching me. I walk back over to him.

"You don't have plans of trying to track mud into the house, do you?"

"No, ma'am. I wouldn't dream of it." But he still has a smile on his face and even with all the mud, he still looks as handsome as ever.

I stalk a little bit closer until I'm close enough, I could reach out and touch him.

"You sure about that? You have that evil look in your eye."

He laughs and reaches out to grab my waist and pulls me in closer.

"I wouldn't dream of making more work for you." He pulls me in as far as he can.

"Is that right?" I say, stepping up on the side of the four-wheeler like I'm going to climb on, but I put my knee on the seat in front of him and put both hands on his shoulders.

He doesn't take his eyes off me. He just tilts his head up to look at me, and I stare down at him. Before I lose my nerve, I lean down and kiss him. I feel one hand move to my leg that's resting on the seat in front of him, and his other hand lands on my waist.

He doesn't pull me in, just holds me steady while he leans in and kisses me back. We hear a few loud whistles, and my brothers call out.

"No PDA! Mudhole rules!" Blaze yells.

"Leave them alone!" I hear Sage yell.

"Make me!" Blaze yells right before I see Sage haul off and throw mud at him, making Riley squeal.

I look back at Hunter, with smiles on our faces.

"Want to get out of here?" he asks.

"Yes, you load up. I'll set up the towels in the truck."

A few minutes later we're back at the barn and the first ones to change and hose ourselves and the four-wheeler off before running back into the house.

After we shower, we both collapse onto the couch.

"Oh, I'm so tired now!" I say and lay my head against the back of the couch.

Hunter sits and pulls my legs onto his lap.

"Me too. I'm thinking we grab lunch then we go upstairs, watch some TV, and nap. Then you can do some studying. I can quiz you and have a study night."

I smile. "Deal, my room or yours?"

Chapter 8

Megan

Graduation is in just a few days, but I just took my last final, and I'm celebrating with the girls tonight! We've kicked all the guys out of the house, and they headed over to Mom and Dad's for the evening. Mom came here.

We haven't had one of these for a while. The last one was when we were doing a makeover on Riley before her first date with Blaze.

Mom has brought her famous brownies, I do everyone's hair, Riley will do nails, and Sage will play DJ and bartender. We just talk or vent and have fun.

"Jason and Mac need to settle down soon. We need some fresh blood for girls night," Sage says.

"I think Mac is talking to someone. I notice him on his phone texting a lot, and he's been very jumpy and hiding his phone. When I ask, he gives me some lame answer like it's his sister or a friend. I don't buy it," Riley says.

Interesting.

"What about Jason? Anyone know if there's anyone in his life?" I ask.

Everyone shakes their heads.

"Hmmm, anyone we can set him up with? I don't remember the last time he was even on a date," I say.

"Oh, you guys need to stop worrying about your brothers. We have bigger things to worry about," Mom says, and we all look at her.

"Like what?" Sage asks.

"Like how long before y'all give me grandbabies! I have one on the way. We need more!"

Riley's eyes go wide, as Sage and I laugh.

"Riley and Blaze just got married. Give them some time, Mom. They can only pop out one at a time, and Sage and Colt haven't even made it down the aisle yet."

Mom pouts. "Well, hurry up. And you need to nail down that boy of yours already."

"Hunter?" I ask.

"Who else?" Sage says.

I feel my cheeks heat up.

Sage continues, "Megs, we all know how Hunter feels about you. The only one who has been blind to it is you. When are you going to open up and let him in?"

I chew on my bottom lip, thinking, *What if it goes all wrong? Not only do I lose my boyfriend but my best friend in one swoop?*

"What if it goes all right, and he's yours forever? You end up with the family and the life you've been dreaming of with your best friend, who knows you better than you know yourself?" Sage counters making me realize I said that out loud.

My heart flutters at that. I want it so bad, I do, but it seems so far out of my reach. Too good to be true.

"That's the dream," I sigh.

"What's holding you back?" Riley asks.

"I just wish I knew that by taking this further it would work out. I'm terrified to lose Hunter."

"Never let the fear of striking out keep you from playing the game," Mom says. It's a saying we heard many times growing up but one I hadn't heard in a while.

"You're both adults. You're making an adult choice, but you can make a promise to not let it affect you if the romantic relationship doesn't work out. You take some time to heal, and the friendship will be there. I bet even stronger," Sage says.

Can I take this chance on us? I want to, and I can't seem to stay away when he's near if the kiss while we were mudding and me crawling into his bed is any indication. The fact he hasn't been with anyone, he's been waiting for me is something I'll keep to myself but no less a huge one.

If he's that sure I'm the one he wants to be with, why can't I be that sure about him? Doesn't he deserve that? I don't want to hurt him; he means so much to me. Then a thought crosses my mind that scares me.

Have I been hurting him all this time by friend-zoning him? That has never been my intention. I've told him I have so much going on with the shop and school, I've wanted to be friends, so I don't hurt him. He has seemed fine with it.

"Megs! Hey, where did you just go?" Sage asks.

"We're taking things slow until after graduation."

"Which is in a few days," Riley says.

"It is. He planned a graduation trip for me. Won't tell me where we're going, but we leave the week after graduation for a week."

That seems to catch everyone's attention, and we spend the next half hour guessing where Hunter might be taking me.

"How are you supposed to know what to pack if he won't tell you?" Sage asks.

"He told me to pack for hot summer weather and make sure to bring a bathing suit."

"Oh, maybe Florida in a sexy beach house?" Riley asks.

"Maybe though that isn't either of our styles. The lake house is fun, but that's as beachy as we get."

"So, maybe it's someplace with a pool or hot tub then?" Sage asks.

"Well, we can rule out the lake house because he said someplace I haven't been."

"Is it out of state?" Mom asks.

"No clue. Again, you know as much as I do."

We end up upstairs in my room picking out summer outfits. Lots of shorts, a few swimsuits, a casual dress, and a dressy dress just in case and shoes to match. This is how the guys find us when they get in, making Hunter laugh.

"Bring in the army to help you pack?" he asks.

"Well, you won't tell me where we're going, so I needed help," I pout.

He looks at my bag. "This is perfect though you don't need the heels or the fancy dress." He takes it out of my bag.

Everyone says good night and slowly files out of my room.

"Do I have everything I'll need packed?"

"Yes, and if we forget anything, we'll be close enough to a store to buy it. I promise."

I sigh. "Okay."

He walks over and wraps his arms around my waist and kisses my temple.

"You're going to love it."

"I know I will. If you planned it, I'm excited to go. I think I'm just nervous about graduation."

We settle on my bed, and the heat of his body next to mine and his hand running up and down my back is so soothing, I don't even remember falling asleep.

Chapter 9

Hunter

Megan is graduating today, in the top five of her class. I couldn't be prouder of her. She's excited because she doesn't have to give a speech.

Ever since that first night she climbed into my bed, we haven't spent a night apart, and I couldn't be happier. Since she had such a hard time sleeping every few hours, she climbs on me, wanting another orgasm. Of course, I'm happy to give them to her. I think I finally get her to pass out around two a.m., just to be back up at it at six a.m. crawling on me again.

Everyone takes their seats, and her family takes up a whole row. I love my girl has such a support system. I check my phone once we sit and see the final confirmation I need for the trip I've planned. I'm excited to have her to myself for a week.

I'll give her this time to celebrate her graduation, but, on this trip, I'm making her mine. I'm not waiting anymore. I've had a sample of her these last few weeks, and now I want the whole thing. I'll do anything to prove to her we're good together, and we can make this work.

When the ceremony starts, I try to pay attention, but the speakers aren't Megan, and they just don't hold my attention, talking about everyone's next steps after today.

When they call everyone's names, I pay attention. They're going in alphabetical order, which means Megan will be in the front.

"Megan Buchanan," the speaker says, and our whole row jumps up, yelling and cheering as she crosses the stage to accept her diploma in her black cap and gown. We all take photos on our phones, and Mom has her professional camera out. I know Jason is recording it as well; he's the one always taking video.

She takes the diploma, shakes the woman's hand, and turns to the crowd, and we all cheer again. The smile on her face is so large, and I know mine matches. Then she makes a silly face, sticking her tongue out before exiting the stage. I can't help but laugh. That's my girl.

Now it feels like I could crawl out of my skin as I wait for everyone else to walk the stage so I can go to my girl and hold her. I don't even realize my legs are bouncing a mile a minute until Riley, who is sitting next to me, puts her hand gently on my knee.

"It won't be much longer now, Hunter," she says softly.

The look on her face has me wondering if she's talking about the graduation ceremony or something more. I don't get to ask because the speaker congratulates everyone and ends the ceremony. I'm up and down the aisle to find Megan before anyone can get another word out.

When I see her, I make a beeline for her, not caring who's in my way. She's talking to another girl in a graduation robe, and I don't even let her finish the conversation before I swoop her into my arms.

"I'm so damn proud of you, Megs," I say and spin her around. The sound of her laughter fills my heart and makes me hard at the same time. I set her down and put my hands on her hips and pull her toward me. I can tell as soon as she feels my erection against her belly because her eyes go wide.

I lean into her ear. "This is what you do to me, baby. Today is the day I stop hiding it. Get ready," I whisper to her ear then pull back just enough to crush her mouth to mine. I move one hand to the back of her neck to deepen the kiss.

The rest of the world falls away, and I don't care that we're standing in the middle of the aisle at her graduation. I don't care that her family will be joining us at any moment. The only thing that matters is my lips are on Megan's, and it feels like heaven.

When Megan grabs hold of my suit coat and pulls me in closer, I can't stop the groan that comes out of me. That's when I hear a few throats being cleared loudly. Reluctantly, I soften the kiss then pull away, wrapping my arms around her. She rests her head on my chest, and that's when I see her family standing behind her.

Sage, Riley, and Megan's mom all smile at me. Blaze and Colt have shit-eating grins, and both wink at me. They've both been in my shoes. Megan's dad has a frown on his face but a smile in his eyes, and he looks anywhere but at us. Jason and Mac just look plain uncomfortable.

I let her go, knowing everyone else will want to congratulate her and take photos with her. I get her mom to snap a few photos of her and me. I want them to remind us of the day everything changed for us. I pick my favorite and save it as my phone background and lock screen.

After what seems like forever, we file out to the parking lot to head back to the ranch, and I pull Megan with me. Before I open the car door, I stop her and turn her to face me.

"I have a gift for you."

"Hunter, I thought the trip was your gift. It's too much!" she says, but her eyes dance with excitement. I know my girl loves gifts.

"I'll always spoil you, Megs, always," I say and reach into my coat jacket to pull out the long velvet box.

I watch her take it and hesitate opening it. When she sees the gift, her eyes tear up, and one hand goes to her mouth.

"It's beautiful, Hunter."

I take the charm bracelet out of the box and secure it on her wrist. Then I turn it to show her the charms.

"The pom poms are for the day I got ditched by the cheerleader, which ended up with me meeting you. The best day of my life, by the way." I look up at her and wink.

"The truck is for all the times we'd just sit under the stars to talk. The 4-wheeler is for all the times we'd go mudding. The cabin is for all the trips to the lake house. The cow is for our first kiss, and the graduation cap is for today. The day I claim you and make you mine. I have the charm to add for the trip, but you'll get that when we get home, so I don't give away the surprise."

When I look up, there are full-on tears running down her cheek. I cup her face and use my thumbs to wipe them away.

"Thank you, Hunter. I love this gift so much. It's perfect."

She stands on her tiptoes and kisses me. Her arms wrap around my neck, and I pin her to the side of the truck. She holds nothing back in this kiss, and I can feel the last of her walls crumbling down. It makes my heart soar, and my soul reaches out to connect with hers.

"You keep kissing me like this, we'll never make it home. I'll pin you down in the back of the truck."

I watch her cheeks turn pink, and it makes me so hard. I rarely see Megan get embarrassed and that flush on her cheeks? I love it there. I pull away and open the truck door for her to get settled.

We head back to the ranch where we're going to celebrate with an afternoon down at the swimming hole. Once at the ranch, we all head in to change before heading out to the swimming hole. Mom, Sage, and Riley have made food and us guys load up the trucks with the floats and coolers of drinks, chairs, and tables.

Once there, we all get set up under the trees. There are some rocks we can jump in from that are about six feet high off the water, or we can go down the hill a bit from where everything is set up and walk right in.

Even as kids, we've always chosen to jump in. Jason and Mac are the first ones in. Sage and Colt follow. Riley and Megan are talking as they remove their swimsuit coverups. When I see Megan in that black bikini, my mouth goes dry, and I'm instantly hard, which is difficult to hide in these swim shorts. I've seen her in her swimsuits before, but today is different.

Today, I'm not forced to keep my mind in the friend zone. Last night, I gave her four orgasms, and I know the face she makes when she comes. Today will be a long day.

Megan catches me looking at her and cocks her head to the side. I stalk over to her, and Riley heads over to Blaze, and they jump in the water next. I stop in front of her and clutch my hands into fists.

"You're playing a dangerous game wearing that today."

Her smirk tells me she knows exactly what she's doing. I whip my shirt off and now it's my turn to watch her eyes go wide and take me in. I can see her nipples harden under her swimsuit, and I'm willing to bet if I reached into those bikini bottoms, she'd be wet for me too. I don't do it though. I take her hand and head to the ledge.

"Ready to jump?" I ask and peek over the side of the rocks to make sure the water is clear, and no one is in our way.

"Let's do it," she says. I count to three, and we both jump and come up to the surface for air without letting go of our hands. I pull her to me and kiss her hard.

"We need to find a spot alone for a bit," I whisper in her ear. I notice Blaze and Colt and their girls have already disappeared. Mac and Jason are lying on rafts tied to the side of the water. She takes my hand, and we swim a little way downstream to a bunch of larger rocks on the side.

She pulls me in and behind one of them. I look around and unless you know where to look, you won't be able to see us with all the boulders blocking the view.

I pin her to one of the boulders and find my feet can touch the bottom, and the water comes up to just below my shoulders still.

Perfect.

I grab her ass and pull her legs around my hips and lean in to kiss her, pressing my erection against her. She runs her hands up my bare chest and then wraps them around my neck, causing my whole body to shiver. I kiss over her jaw and down her neck, learning the spots she reacts to and lightly scraping my teeth along her neck.

I trail my hands up her sides and stop at the bottom of her bikini top. I kiss her collarbone, and she wraps her hands in my hair. She wiggles her hips against mine, causing my whole body to explode in little lightning shocks.

I rub my thumbs on the underside of her breasts over the swimsuit top, causing her to moan.

"More, Hunter."

I trail my kisses back up to her mouth and hover there. "Tell me you're mine, Megan. That this is our start. No more friend zone, no more pushing me away."

"Hunter..."

"It's okay to be scared. I'm scared too, but I need you to be mine, Megan. Be mine. Mine. Say it," I say between kisses, short ones just enough to drive her crazy.

"I'm yours, Hunter. Always have been."

I growl then I can't stop myself as I reach up and pull her swim top to the side, exposing both breasts and stare at the most perfect pair of tits I've ever seen.

"You're so damn beautiful," I tell her before leaning down and taking one nipple in my mouth, sucking it hard, and swirling my tongue around the hard nub. I let it go with a pop and take the second one in my mouth, giving it the same treatment.

I slowly kiss my way back to the first nipple and slide my hand down her stomach at the same time. My hand stops and traces the top of her bikini bottoms while my tongue circles her nipple. I gently run my teeth over the tight peak before dipping my hand down and running my fingers over her slit.

She throws her head back against the rock and moans. Even though we're in the water, I can tell she's soaking wet. I circle her clit with my thumb before slowly pushing my middle finger inside her. She's so tight. I move slow, so I don't hurt her.

I pull back so I can see her face and watch her reaction. Her hips buck the harder I circle her clit, and it makes it easier to thrust my finger in and out of her. She has a death grip on my hair, and I love it. After a few more thrusts, I work a second finger into her.

"You're so tight, baby. It feels so good just having my fingers in you. I can only imagine once my cock is inside this tight little body."

I feel her pussy spasm, and I smile. "Like the dirty talk, do you, Megs?"

"Oh God, Hunter. I'm so close."

"I can feel you are, baby. Come for me. Come all over my hand."

I press harder on her clit and curl my finger up, looking for that spot inside her. When her thighs clamp around me, I know I found it. I take her mouth with mine to muffle her screams, and I feel a gush of warmth around my hand. I don't stop thrusting my finger until her body relaxes.

When I take my fingers out of her, she opens her eyes to look at me. I bring my fingers to my mouth and suck them clean. Even being in the water, there's still the slight taste of her on them, and it causes my cock to jerk against her already tender clit.

She gasps and then reaches a hand into my shorts and grips my hard length, causing me to groan.

"You don't have to do this, Megs."

"You got to watch me come. I think it's only fair I get the same experience," she whispers.

I won't ever deny her what she wants, and she already knows this. I look into her eyes, never breaking eye contact, and she strokes me.

"Harder, baby," I let out in a strangled whisper. Her grip on me tightens, and it only takes a few more strokes before I'm coming. I bite the inside of my cheek to keep quiet, and my hands squeeze her hips so hard, I'm sure I'm going to leave a bruise.

When she has worked the last of my cum from me, I open my eyes and see a smile on her face.

"That was amazing, Megs."

"Hmm, it was."

"We need to get back before they notice we're gone."

"I don't want to move," she pouts. "I don't think I can move."

I laugh. "Wrap your arms around my neck. I got you, baby."

She does, and I take a moment to adjust our swimsuits before leaving our spot in the rocks.

We slip back to the main swimming area at the same time Blaze and Riley do. Blaze gives me a knowing smirk when he sees Megan clinging to me, and I give him one back when I see the flush covering Riley.

We all laugh and talk for a while, swimming before getting out and having dinner, and watching the sunset. It's the perfect ending to the day that is the start of the rest of my life.

Chapter 10

Hunter

Tonight, I'm having dinner with my parents. We do dinner once a week, but they like to eat early. Then I'm able to head to Megan's to eat with her and her family. I fill up at Mom's and just eat a smaller portion at the ranch. If they've noticed, they never say anything.

My parents live on the edge of town. They own the property the vet clinic is on and the hundred acres behind it. They live on the far end, away from the clinic, so they have some privacy. Dad has a road he drives from the clinic to the house, so he never has to leave the property.

Mom has a few horses in the barn, but the property is mostly used to house animals they rescue until they get them new homes. It's also used to watch animals under our care at the clinic. Mom has rescued lots of horses and dogs. Dad has taken on a few bulls after a rodeo injury. We even had a monkey here once that was confiscated until it was sent to a rescue.

I loved growing up around all the animals. It just fueled my passion to be a vet like Dad. I'd always spend time after school at the clinic with him, and Mom would make me spend one day at home on the weekends learning to cook, clean, do chores, and do yard work. The other day was spent helping Dad with house calls.

Dad has been friends with Megan's dad for years and has been out on his ranch several times before she and I met. I was surprised we hadn't crossed paths before that day I met her at Cindy's house.

My parents like Megan and her whole family, so they never mind when I spend so much time over there. I have told Dad how I feel about her once, and it's like he's known she's my forever before I do.

I park my car in the driveway and look at the house I grew up in. It hasn't changed much other than the landscaping. Every few years, Mom likes to change up the flowers and add new colors to the house. Right now, it's in shades of purples and oranges with a few yellows. Last time it was reds, pinks, white.

When they got back from their Hawaii vacation ten years ago it was all bright pinks, yellows, oranges, and reds.

I walk up the front porch and don't even bother knocking on the door.

"Mom! Dad!" I call out.

"Kitchen, son," Dad calls back.

I take my shoes off in the entryway and make my way to the back of the house and into the kitchen. Dad is helping Mom by chopping vegetables, and I love seeing them work in the kitchen together. Dad also makes it a point to be home for dinner. Family dinner has always been a non-negotiable. Dad has had times where an animal emergency pulled him away, but otherwise, every night we're all at the table. As a teenager, with after-school activities and dating, I was home at least once a week for dinner. Morning family breakfasts before school soon became a tradition instead.

I lean in and kiss Mom on the cheek and then pat Dad on the back.

"Hunter! How was Megan's graduation? We need to have her over soon. It's been too long!" Mom says.

"It was good. I don't remember much other than her crossing the stage, but I have pictures."

"Oh, let us just get this in the oven, and you can show us," Mom says.

"Also remember I won't be here next week. I'm taking Megan on a road trip to celebrate her graduation. She was in the top five people in her class."

"We'll miss you, son, but she has studied hard and deserves a break, just like you," Dad says.

"You sure you'll be okay at the clinic?"

"Oh yes, your mom will come in help like she used to. It's been a while since we worked together, so I'm rather looking forward to it."

That makes me smile. They make a great team.

Once dinner is in the oven, we sit in the living room to show them pictures of Megan's graduation, and we talk about her taking over the beauty shop and my plans for the trip. We talk about Sage and Colt's upcoming wedding even about work at the clinic before we sit to eat dinner.

"This is really good, Mom."

"Thanks, it's a new recipe. Well new to me; it's a traditional meatloaf and the veggies we needed to use up. I know cornbread is your favorite."

"Well, this recipe is a keeper," I say.

"I second that," Dad says.

"How are things going living out on the ranch?" Mom asks. They tried to get me to move home when they found out I was moving to the ranch, but I had to explain it wasn't because I couldn't find a place it was because I wanted to be closer to Megan to win her over.

"It's going well. It's a bit longer of a drive into work, and they're up a bit earlier than I normally would be, but there's always someone there. I find I don't miss the quiet."

"You always were a people person. It's not too cramped with eight of you now living there?" Mom asks.

"Mom, you've seen the house. We wouldn't be cramped if there were twenty of us there. We don't even take up half the bedrooms. It's easy to get privacy if you want it, but we all get along so well we tend to gravitate to each other anyway."

The ranch house is huge. It's a mansion really and it was Sage's family's home but when her bio dad went to jail for abusing her, her bio mom couldn't keep up with it. The family banded together and bought it right after Megan graduated high school. They combined it with the land Megan's family already had and they are now the second biggest ranch in the state of Texas.

Sage had the house completely remodeled and then moved her, Megan, and their brothers into it. Riley now lives there with Blaze and Sage and Colt are in the master. The house is so big it has fourteen bedrooms upstairs and is split into the family wing and the guest wing. Downstairs has a whole one-bedroom apartment for the housekeeper, but Sage has yet to hire one. They seem to make do. Sage even has a room set up like a big playroom that can also be used as a schoolroom once everyone has kids. She planned everything when she remodeled the house. It looks nothing like it did when she was a kid.

Their parents' home on the east side of the property is just as big. More than half the house doesn't get used anymore but is set up for guests or any of the kids if needed. Like when Riley's ex broke into the house to try to attack her. Everyone stayed with their parents until the house was cleaned and the window fixed.

I love the property and the house so being able to live there means a lot to me, but I don't know how to make my parents understand that without hurting them. They love the land they own, and I do too, but the ranch is important to Megan, so that makes it important to me.

We eat in silence for a minute before I speak, "So, Megan and I've been moving forward in our relationship."

"Finally!" Mom says, and Dad just chuckles.

"We're taking it slow, but I told her I'd give her until graduation, then I told her she was mine. She didn't fight me." I leave out the part that I'm withholding an orgasm from her until she agreed. There are just some things parents don't need to know.

"Do you have a plan for this trip?" Dad asks.

"To show her I can be the best damn boyfriend and partner she has ever dreamed of." That includes plenty of orgasms and holding her in my arms every night and finding the perfect time to tell her I love her.

"That's all you can do," Dad says.

I look down at my plate then back up at them.

"She's it for me. This is the girl I'm going to marry. I know it in my heart, and if I have to keep taking it slow, I will. If she were ready to walk down the aisle tomorrow, I'd be there and ready."

Neither of them says anything; they just look at me then at each other.

"Well, only time will tell now. Don't push her too fast," Mom says.

Mom changes the subject and tells me about the rescue horse she just got in and how she's thinking of having Sage work with it a bit since he's a bit skittish right now.

As I head home, I can't keep Megan off my mind. I'll move as slow as she wants, but that doesn't mean it'll be easy.

Chapter 11

Megan

Today we're heading out on our trip, and I'm so excited, even though Hunter had me up at the crack of dawn. He says we have a twelve-hour drive ahead of us, and I ask why we aren't flying. He says he has always wanted to take a road trip with me. So here we are, on the road at five a.m., coffee in one hand and his hand in the other, and I'm not even complaining.

We're heading northwest so my mind races with everything we could be doing, but there's so much on the list. I decide to wait until we get a bit closer before I guess.

Around nine a.m., I see signs for Amarillo before we start to head west, and then get off the interstate.

Hunter smiles. "This is just a pit stop."

A few minutes later, we pull into Cadillac Ranch. Once we park, Hunter pulls a few cans of spray paint out of the back, and we head over to leave our mark on the Cadillac cars sticking out of the dirt.

We spray paint each other's names and a few cute designs before we end with our names in a heart. We meet a nice couple with a few small kids who take our photo next to our names before we leave and continue west.

I'm looking through the photos smiling.

"Thank you. I loved that stop."

"I knew you would. Also welcome to Old Route 66. We'll be on it for most of the rest of the day."

I get excited. We've always talked about driving down Route 66. As we head west toward Albuquerque, New Mexico, we stop at a small vintage Route 66 diner for lunch.

"I love this place!" I say, taking in the old neon signs and vintage Route 66 décor. The tables and booths all look new but have the old retro vibe. They even have an old soda fountain.

"Let's hope you love the food."

"Well, I don't think this place would still be around if the food sucked."

"Very true." He looks at the menu and reaches out across the table to take my hand.

The waitress comes up to take our drink order. She's in a vintage waitress uniform in pale pink with a white lace apron.

"Two sweet ice teas, hers with three lemon slices," Hunter orders.

I smile that he knows my drink order, and he doesn't flinch when ordering.

"What you in the mood for?" he asks.

"I don't know. The fried chicken looks good, but the BLT sounds good too with the herbed mayo."

When the waitress brings us our drinks and asks about our order, he doesn't hesitate.

"I'll take the fried chicken platter with mac and cheese, and she will do the BLT with no tomato and extra of the mayo on the side with fries."

When the waitress walks away, he looks back at me and seems to get uncomfortable.

"What's wrong?"

"How do you do that?"

"Do what?"

"Know exactly what I want. Has it always been this way, and I just overlooked it?"

He looks down at the table, and his hand still holding mine trembles a bit.

"I spent these last few years getting to know everything about you. I hid how well I knew you, but I'm obsessed with you. Every little thing about you drives me crazy in the best possible way. I told you I'm not holding back anymore."

Most women might get scared when he says he's obsessed with me. Most women might not be okay with him ordering for them. I'm not most women, because those things? They turn me on, so much so I have to clench my thighs together because my pussy is pulsing with need for him.

"Well, I don't want you holding back anymore. I want to know all of it. Give me all of you this week, Hunter, just you and me."

His eyes meet mine, and I see relief there and something short of love.

"You have all of me, Megan, always."

Our food comes, and he takes half my sandwich and gives me half of his fried chicken—the dark meat, of course. He also splits the side dishes before we dig in.

"This food is good," I say.

"Yeah, definitely worth the stop."

Then something crosses my mind.

"You ordered the fried chicken because I couldn't choose. If you were here without me, what would you've ordered?"

He smiles. "The fried chicken."

I look at him. I know he likes fried chicken, but does he like it only because I do? Is he being honest with me or telling me what I want to hear?

"What's going on in that head of yours, Megs?"

"Is that true or are you telling me what I want to hear?"

He sets his fork down and wipes his mouth with his napkin before his eyes meet mine.

"Have I ever lied to you?"

I stop and think. Has he? No. He's been brutally honest sometimes, but I don't think he has ever lied to me.

"No. Not that I know of."

"That's because I haven't. I won't either. I've seen lies destroy relationships, and you mean more to me than that. I love fried chicken, always have."

"Okay." What else can I say? We finish our lunches, and he orders us two milkshakes to go. Birthday cake for me and cherry for him.

We keep heading west, passing through Albuquerque, and crossing into Arizona. We make a stop in Holbrook, Arizona to see the famous Wigwam Motel on Route 66 and then also stop in Winslow, Arizona to get our photo at the Standin' on A Corner in Winslow

Arizona park made famous by the Eagles' song.

Looking around after we have our photos, the whole section of town is Route 66 everything. It's painted on the street and the benches, and signs in the old neon.

"I love this. It's everything I thought of when I pictured Route 66."

I say as we walk back to our car. Hunter wraps his arm around my waist.

"Me too." He kisses my temple and helps me back in the truck.

We continue west towards Flagstaff, and now I'm getting curious.

"How much longer of a drive do we have?" I ask.

"A little less than two hours. You okay to wait until we get there for dinner, or do you want to eat now?" he takes my hand.

"I can wait."

We pass time by reading all the old signs and taking in the Route 66 stops. Once we hit Flagstaff, he turns south. A few minutes later, he gets off the main highway.

"Taking the scenic route," he says. That's when it hits me.

"Sedona?!" I ask and watch his face break out into a huge smile.

"Sedona," he confirms.

I can't believe he remembered. A few years ago, I was flipping through my Facebook feed and saw some pictures of Sedona. We were at his place, sitting on the couch, and we looked it up. I remember being in awe of the red rocks. I said I'd love to visit one day. That day is today.

I lean over the center console and kiss him on the cheek. "I can't believe you remembered. Thank you, it's perfect."

He rolls down the windows and cranks up the music as we drive along a river, taking in the Red Rock Mountains before getting to Sedona. Even from the downtown area, you can see the Red Rocks all around. He stops at a restaurant on the edge of downtown.

"I rented us a cabin. I thought we could have dinner here, stop at the store, and pick up some things to head in for the night?"

I smile. "It's perfect."

Dinner is amazing, even though when I tried to get some of Hunter's plans out of him, he wouldn't share. He does ask what I want to do while I'm here.

Chapter 12

Hunter

It was a long drive yesterday, but road tripping with Megan was everything I always imagined it would be. She was fun and up for any stop. She made the time pass by fast.

After getting into the cabin with her, we put the food away and look around. We have a hot tub and our own private deck with killer views of the Red Rock Mountains. And complete privacy. But I think the best part is being able to convince Megan to share the master bedroom with me.

Falling asleep with her in my arms is a close tie to waking up with her in my arms. Add in this is happening every day for a week, and I'm in pure heaven.

Megan is still peacefully asleep when I slip from bed and head to the kitchen to make her breakfast. A western omelet, bacon, and coffee. I'm just plating the food when I hear her enter the kitchen.

"This smells so good. One of the best things, when I was living with you a few months ago, was your food. Don't tell Sage or Mom, but you're a better cook."

I had loved when Megan was living with me then. It was because Riley's crazy Ex has found out where she was and had resisted arrest. He had drugs and unregistered guns in his house, so her brothers didn't want her at the house until he was caught. I almost begged her to move in with me for good then. I laugh. "Your secret is safe with me." I kiss her cheek and have her sit while I make her coffee.

When I bring the food over to her, and we start eating, she asks, "What's on the agenda today?"

"Well, I booked us a pink jeep tour around town this morning, and I figured this afternoon we could decide from there where you want to explore some more."

"Which tour are we taking?"

I pull up my phone and check the name. "It's an ancient ruins tour. It's a dig site with Native American homes built into the rock that date back seven hundred years. I guess they take a scenic route there and back and have a certified guide for the ruins tour."

"Oh my God, Hunter. That sounds amazing!" I can tell she's excited; she's bouncing in her seat, which makes me smile.

"Okay, well, eat up. We need to get ready to make the tour."

Once we get to the tour office, we discover that we're the only two on the tour today, so I'm excited. We get out to the jeep, and the driver is a very friendly woman in her fifties.

"You two make such a cute couple. Are you here celebrating anything special?" she asks.

"Well, we are. My girlfriend here just graduated with her business degree, and she was one of the top five in her class. It's time to relax and celebrate before she takes over the business world," I say and ignore the fact that Megan tenses when I use the word girlfriend.

When I look down at her, she's smiling, and I guess she isn't having second thoughts about it.

The tour is so much fun seeing everything up close and getting a private tour of the ruins. The drive there and back is great too.

After the tour, we have a small lunch, and Megan wants to drive around town a bit. We stop at a few small shopping centers and walk the stores. There are a lot of arts and crafts to take in. We pick up a few dreamcatchers for the house.

Mac, Megan's youngest brother, is from the local Native American reservation. When he was adopted, their parents promised the tribal leaders they would keep his heritage alive. They have, and the family has a great relationship with the tribe.

Sage loves getting different dreamcatchers for around the house and as she travels, she picks up many from different tribes across the country. While here, Megan wants to help her add to the collection.

She picks out one that has the same colors as the Red Rocks behind it and another that matches the colors of Sage's office. She picks up one for Mac too that has a wolf in the center. He has this thing with wolves, so I know he'll like it.

Walking around hand in hand, I let her drag me in and out of every store in the town, and I happily carry her bags. I know most guys would be bored to death, but I've waited so long for this. I don't want it to ever end.

That night, we grab takeout from a place in town and head back to the cabin. We sit out on the back deck and watch the sunset over the mountains while we eat.

"Tomorrow, I was thinking we head out to Jerome. It's a ghost town about an hour from here up on the mountains. It's supposed to be a beautiful drive."

"Sounds good. Today was perfect, Hunter. Thank you for this trip. I love being here with you and just relaxing."

"Anything for you, Megs. What do you think of taking advantage of the hot tub tonight?"

I watch her eyes light up. "That sounds perfect."

We finish dinner and head up to change into our swimsuits. When Megan comes out of the bathroom in a navy blue bikini with white dots, I'm instantly hard and having a hard time remembering why I wanted to even leave the bedroom, to begin with.

Megan seems to be having just as hard of a time wanting to leave as she takes me in with my swim shorts and nothing else. I know she can see how hard I am from where she's standing. There's no hiding it.

"Megan baby, if you want to actually make it to the hot tub, you need to stop staring at me like that and move your sexy butt out of this room," I say in a very husky tone.

That seems to catch her attention as she jumps and rushes from the room. I reach down to adjust myself and follow behind her. The view of her from behind is just as sexy as the front, and I can feel the cum leaking from my cock.

I grab a couple of towels and pour us each a glass of wine before meeting her out on the deck. Megan is already in the water, looking so relaxed. I set the towels down and hand her both glasses of wine as I climb in.

When I sit, she hands me my glass, and I hold it up. "To you Megs, I'm so damn proud of everything you've done and worked for. I can't wait to see where you take that shop."

I watch her eyes mist over, and we clink our glasses and take a sip. I watch her over the rim of my glass as she slowly sips the wine. The way her lips slip over the edge of the wine glass. The way her pink tongue darts off, getting every drop from her lips, and the way the slender column of her neck moves as she swallows it down.

I can't take it anymore, I need to touch her. I set my glass on the side of the hot tub and then take her glass to set it next to mine. I grab her around the waist and pull her into my lap. She's straddling me with her legs on the sides of my hips when I lean in to kiss her.

I taste the wine on her lips, and my head goes fuzzy as if I'm drunk just from this kiss. My hands on her bare skin at her hips tingle, and I bring one up to her hair and pull her in to deepen the kiss. When my tongue meets hers, her hips jerk against mine, causing me to groan.

I trail kisses down her neck, and she leans her head back, giving me more room. I kiss down to the straps holding the top of her bikini, and I pull back slowly, bringing my hand up to where the top is tied and looking her in the eye. Silently asking for permission to untie the knot. When she nods her head, I take a deep breath and untie the top. It falls between us, causing her plump breasts to spring free.

"Megan..." I groan. "God, your tits are perfect," I whisper as I reach up and take one in each hand. I test their weight and run a thumb over each nipple, causing her to gasp. I bring my mouth up to one, suck her nipple into my mouth, and lightly bite down on it. When her hips jerk against mine again, I grin. This time she continues to grind on me.

"That's it, baby, take what you need," I say then bring her other nipple to my mouth and give it the same treatment.

"Megan baby, can I taste you?" I ask. All I can think about is getting my mouth on her.

She hesitantly nods, and I move quickly, setting her on the edge of the hot tub where she can lean her back against the porch rail. I spread her legs wide and untie the sides of her bottoms and get my first look at her beautiful pink pussy.

"So beautiful, Megs," I whisper before leaning in and giving a firm lick from her slit to her clit. She tastes like heaven and cherries. Her hips thrust into my face, so I grab her hips to hold her steady as I suck on her clit.

I circle her clit with my tongue and play with it before licking back down and thrusting my tongue inside of her. Her legs shake, so I move back to licking her clit and trail one hand from her hip across her thigh and down to her pussy. I slide it up and down her lips before sliding a finger inside her.

She's so wet and tight, and the thought of her this wet and tight on my cock has cum dripping down my cock. I lazily thrust my finger in and out of her while I suck hard on her clit. She brings her hands down and knots them in my hair, pulling me closer. She keeps moaning my name, and I know she's close, so I give her clit a gentle nip followed by a hard suck, and she explodes on my tongue.

I suck up every drop of her release like my life depends on it. Having her come on my tongue is enough to have me come in my pants. God, you would think I'd have a bit more self-control than this, but I don't even care. I could do this all day for the rest of my life.

I'd happily come in my pants over and over again if it means my Megan comes on my tongue like she did.

When she relaxes, I retie her bikini bottoms, grasp her hips, slide her back into the hot water, and pull her on to my lap. I fix her swimsuit top. She rests her head on my shoulder and lets out a satisfied sigh that makes my heart swell. A minute later, she sits up and looks at me.

"Your turn." She tries to reach for me.

I grab her hand. "No need, baby."

"I want to, Hunter."

I smile. "I know you do, baby, but you coming on my tongue was the hottest, sexiest thing I've ever seen, so much so I came in my pants when you did."

I watch a smile creep across her face. "I like that I can do that to you."

I kiss the tip of her nose. "I like that you can do that to me too."

We finish our wine, then I carry her back to our room, where she dries off and gets in bed. Ending the night with her in my arms and a huge smile on my face.

Chapter 13

Megan

Today, we're exploring Jerome, Arizona. An hour's drive away, we drive up the mountain, which offers some amazing views back toward Sedona. There are some people still living near the town but for the most part, the area is deserted.

The guy who owned the mine back in its heyday had a mansion built with killer views, and that's now the museum for the history of the area. We bring a lunch and take advantage of the picnic area out front with the views.

Then we head back toward Sedona and take some scenic roads just driving to see what we can find. We go out to dinner and walk some of the shops again. Hunter holds my hand the entire time, and it just feels right.

Going to bed and falling asleep in his arms is the perfect end to the day.

• • • • • • • • • •

I wake up again today to him making me breakfast. This time it's French toast, and man is it good.

"Make sure to put your swimsuit on under your clothes today," he says, and that catches my attention.

"Where are we going?"

"It's a surprise. Pack extra clothes and grab some towels. We'll head to town, get takeout for lunch, and hit the road."

Now I'm excited. I get ready in record time, and Hunter laughs as he grabs clothes. We load up the truck and head into town to grab lunch from this deli one of the shop owners told us about last night.

Then we head back down the road we came into town on. I can't get over how beautiful this area is. This road is labeled one of the most scenic in the country if I remember correctly.

We pull into Slide Rock State Park. We saw this place on the way here. Even the parking area backs up to some of the Red Rock Mountains.

We grab our lunch and head in. There's a huge grassy area we spread out our blanket and pull out our lunch.

We lay out enjoying the view and end up in a game of this or that, seeing if we know each other like we think we do.

"Pizza or tacos?" I ask Hunter.

He laughs. "Always tacos, for you too."

"I knew that." I smile proudly.

"Okay, cats or dogs?" he asks next.

"You love all animals, but you would pick dogs just like me. They cuddle and are more interactive. Unless it's for the barn, then definitely cats."

"Exactly. You're next."

I think hard. "Oh! I got it. What's worse, laundry or dishes?"

He laughs. "I don't mind dishes. I know you hate them, so I'll do all the dishes while you watch TV and fold laundry."

"You are the perfect man." I laugh.

"Pancakes or waffles?"

What a trick question. "Neither. French toast."

He laughs. "Good answer." Then he shifts and pulls me to sit between his legs, so my back is pressed to his chest, and wraps his arms around my waist.

"Mountains or the beach?"

He nuzzles the side of my neck. "The ranch with you. But if we're going on vacation, the mountains."

I lean my head back on his shoulder. He knows just what to say, so I have to be sure. "You aren't saying what I want to hear, are you?"

"No, I promise you. I guess I've spent so much time around you, I've come to love what you do because you're there. Now a card or a board game?"

"Board games most days. TV or Books?"

"I'd watch TV while you're curled up in my arms reading whatever book you and Sage are currently swapping."

I laugh aloud. "Sounds perfect. Tell me about your perfect date."

"This."

"Hunter..."

"No really. Just being with you, relaxing, good food, good scenery. I have you in my arms. We're talking, maybe a little kissing. This is my perfect date."

I close my eyes to get my emotions in check. If I weren't already sitting down, I'm sure I would have just swooned. Do women still do that? My eyes are misty, and I know at this moment my heart is full. This is where I want to be. In his arms.

When I open my eyes, I look up to see him watching me. I wrap one arm around his neck behind me and pull him in for a kiss. I meant for it to be a quick, light, sweet kiss, but the moment his lips touch mine, Hunter deepens the kiss, and my body feels like it's on fire.

I forget where we are but thankfully, Hunter doesn't. He pulls back just enough to murmur on my lips, "Little kids around. Don't want to take it too much further." He gives me one more quick, soft kiss before pulling back. "Ready to go swimming?" he asks.

All I can do is nod; I'm still breathless from that kiss.

Hunter packs everything up and runs back to grab our towels. We walk the property a bit to find a small open-air museum dedicated to the farm that used to be on this site.

We make our way down to the river, and this is the main event. The rocks have formed a natural slide in the river here, and it's now a great swimming hole among the red rocks. There's a lifeguard stand and everything here.

We spend the next few hours having fun on the natural slide and taking in the refreshing river. But something about seeing the water drip off Hunter has my whole body on fire.

"You ready to head back?" I ask.

"Yeah, you sure?"

"Yeah," I say, wrapping the towel around me, hoping he doesn't notice how turned on I am by watching him. We head back to the car, slip on our clothes, and head back to the cabin.

When we walk in, I take a deep breath and go for what I want.

"I'm going to take a shower," I say, and I watch the heat in his eyes.

"Okay, I'll take one when you get out."

"Or... you can join me," I say barely above a whisper.

"You sure?" he asks, but I see him clench his fists like he's trying not to reach out for me.

I turn to walk toward the bedroom but stop and look over my shoulder. His eyes are planted on my ass.

"You coming?" I ask.

"No, but *you* will be," he growls and follows me into the bathroom, making me laugh.

I turn the water on so it can heat up and turn to face Hunter as we face each other and slowly strip our clothes off while the other one watches. Shirts, pants, and swimsuits end up on the ground, and we just stand there, taking each other in.

It's the first time we've been completely naked in front of each other, and neither of us seems to be the one to want to move first and break the spell.

"Damn, Megan, you're so fucking sexy. I'm the luckiest man in the world to be here with you."

I shake my head. "Hunter, I was just thinking the same thing. Your body is perfect." I step forward, place my hand on his chest, and slowly trace down his abs. His hands come to my hips, and he leans in to kiss me soft and tender.

He backs me into the shower, and the water hitting us doesn't stop our kiss. He slides his hands up my sides and cups my breasts, giving them a firm squeeze.

"Oh God, Hunter."

"You like that, baby?"

I groan as he takes my mouth with his again before pulling back and grabbing my body wash. He washes every inch of me, paying special attention to my breasts, pussy, and ass. When he's done, I return the favor but when I try to take him in my mouth, he stops me and ends the shower.

He dries me off then gets a little shy.

"What's wrong?" I ask.

"I was wondering if you would sleep in bed with me like this. I want to hold you, skin to skin."

I run my hand over his chest and watch goosebumps form. Knowing I have that effect on this sexy alpha man gives me the courage to say yes.

We climb into bed and cuddle up in the dark room. I run my fingers over his abs, something I don't realize I'm doing until he brings his hand up to intertwine my fingers in his.

I'm going to miss this when we get home. The thought crashes into me, and the thought of not being in bed with him when we get home isn't one I like. Even sleeping in my bed is too far away from the man I love.

Whoa. I love Hunter?

I love Hunter.

I'm in love with Hunter.

This thought makes my heart race, and I have the urge to tell him right now. I don't think I can look at him again and not say it.

I sit up on my elbow and look down at him. There's enough light in the room I can see him staring back at me, but neither of us say anything. I think the darkness gives me the courage to make the leap.

I rest my hand on the side of his face. "I love you, Hunter."

I watch his eyes go wide, and I hear the sharp intake of breath as he closes his eyes.

"Say it again?" he asks, and it makes me smile.

"I love you, Hunter."

He opens his eyes and stares into mine.

"I love you too, Megan, so damn much," he says before flipping me over, and his mouth crashes into mine.

The kiss is so full of love and passion, I can tell he's been holding back, not wanting to scare me off. He kisses down my neck while I run my hands through his hair.

He slides his hands up my sides and cups my breasts, pinching the nipples. It causes my back to arch, and I can feel how hard he is.

I take his face in my hand and pull him up to me.

"I want you, Hunter." I watch as he closes his eyes.

"Are you sure, Megan?" he asks, but his voice is strained. "I'm okay to wait."

"We've waited long enough, don't you think? I love you, and I've never been surer of anything in my life. I want you, here, tonight."

He takes a deep breath and takes my lips in a slow kiss before pulling back again.

"Will you trust me to make this good for you, for us?" he asks in a whisper against my lips.

"I trust you, Hunter."

He kisses me again, but this time I feel his hard length glide against my clit.

"Hunter!"

"I've got you, baby. Come for me."

His erection keeps stroking my clit, and the buildup is fast and furious and hits me before I even know what's going on. I can only scream his name as he keeps stroking me. Then I feel his warm cum on my belly.

Chapter 14

Hunter

I'm shaking, and I can't seem to stop it. Megan underneath me naked is almost more than I can take.

"You okay?" she whispers.

"Yeah, baby." I kiss her again. I lean down and pick up my shirt from the floor with the intent of cleaning her off, but seeing her with my come on her is enough to make me hard again.

I clean her up and lean down this time to suck on her clit. I want her to come for me again. I think I'm becoming addicted to making her come. Is that a thing? Do they have support groups?

"Hunter, Hunter, Hunter…" she chants my name and grips my hair. I love every minute of it. My tongue circles her clit, sucking hard, and she comes apart for me again. Her thighs clamp around my head, and I draw out her climax as long as I can.

When she's finally relaxed, I kiss my way up her body again and brace myself over her on my arms by her head. My heart races so fast, I wonder if she can hear it. Her eyes lock with mine and for a moment, neither of us speak.

"You sure about this, Megs?"

"Yes, Hunter. I want you. I love you."

"I love you too, baby." I get the condoms from my bag. I hadn't planned for this, but I still want to be prepared.

I get the condom on, climb back over her, and position myself at her entrance.

"Keep your eyes on mine, Megan," I say, and she nods. Keeping my eyes on her, I slowly slide into her. She's hot and wet and feels like heaven, and I'm only an inch in. She shifts her hips, and I pause.

"You okay?" I ask.

"Yes, just go slow."

I nod and take a deep breath. I slowly slide in and hit her resistance.

"I'm so sorry this is going to hurt you baby, but I promise to make it better."

She nods. "I trust you, Hunter."

I pull back slowly and thrust forward a bit harder and feel myself breaking through the barrier of her virginity and slide in. Megan lets out a small squeal of pain and her body tenses. I wrap my arms around her shoulders and bury my head in her neck.

"You feel amazing, Megan. I love you so much. Thank you for this; you're perfect," I whisper.

I feel her relax, and I slowly thrust until I'm fully inside her.

"You okay?" I ask, pausing.

"It feels good, Hunter; don't stop."

I try not to focus on the sensations washing over me and how every nerve in my body is coming alive. I'm determined to make this beautiful girl come again. I don't want her to remember the pain from this moment.

I lean down to kiss her and reach between us to rub my thumb over her clit, and her hips jerk.

"Hunter... I'm close."

"Good, baby, so am I. Come for me. I want you to know that during our first time, you came all over my cock for me."

I press a bit harder on her clit, and her body locks ups. She digs her nails into my back and screams my name as she comes for me. Feeling her pussy grab my cock is all I can take. I come so hard, I can't catch my breath.

Nothing in my life has ever felt this good. I've never come so hard or so long; it's like I can't stop.

Once I finally catch my breath, I roll off her, so I don't crush her and pull her into my arms.

"Wow, Hunter."

I kiss the top of her head. "Yeah, wow." I get up and take care of the condom. I see the streaks of her virgin blood on it, and I can't help but smile. She gave me this amazing gift tonight. I get a warm washcloth to clean her up. I know she'll be sore for a few days.

I crawl into bed with her and pull her into my arms. "I can't tell you what it means for you to give yourself to me tonight, Megs," I say but get a bit choked up.

"Hunter, I know how you feel. I feel the same way that you gave yourself to me. I'm so glad you waited for me; that is the most amazing gift."

I wrap her up in a tight hug, and we both drift off to sleep.

• • • • • • • • •

Megan

I wake up to delicious soreness between my legs and instantly flashback to last night. It was perfect. Hunter was perfect. I look over at Hunter, and he's still sleeping on his side, facing me with an arm around my stomach. The day I met him, I thought he was the most gorgeous boy I ever saw. Even now, I still think he's the most gorgeous man I've ever seen.

I look at his bare chest and no matter how much I've seen it, it still draws me in. He has abs but not the abs you get from a gym, doing the perfect exercises. Hunter's are hard-earned from doing manual labor, visiting all the ranches he does for work, and helping at the ranch with my family. Somehow, that makes them sexier.

I run my fingers down the grooves of his abs, tracing each one. I only get about halfway through when he stirs, and his hand grabs mine.

"Morning, beautiful," he mumbles as he wakes up. I notice his erection tenting the sheets, and I try to run my hand down to it, but he stops me.

"I know you're sore, baby."

"That doesn't mean I can't have fun with you."

"As much as I love that idea, I'm not coming if you aren't. I was thinking maybe we go for a drive today. Go check out the Chapel of the Holy Cross and some of the other stops we haven't seen yet?"

"Mmm, sounds good. Maybe some hot tub time tonight?"

"Anything you want." He leans in to kiss me.

We spend the day around town, just going with the flow. We check out a winery and visit the Chapel of the Holy Cross. It's this amazing church built into the side of the Sedona Red Rocks. Not only is the church beautiful, but it also has some amazing views too.

We eat both lunch and dinner out and stay to listen to some live music before coming back to the cabin.

"Still up for the hot tub?" I ask.

"Yeah, let's get changed."

"No need," I say and strip out of my clothes on the way to the hot tub, leaving a trail of clothes like breadcrumbs.

"Megan..." I hear him growl behind me, but I don't have to look over my shoulder to know he's following me.

I barely make it into the hot tub before his hands are on me, pulling me into his lap. I take him by surprise when I straddle him and sink onto his hard length.

He groans and throws his head back.

As I slide back up, he says, "Shit, baby... condom."

I don't move and say, "I've been on the pill for years but if you want me to stop, I will."

"Fuck no, it feels too damn good. You sure about this?"

"With you, yes."

He was sure about me too because he didn't let me out of the hot tub until I'd come three times for him.

Chapter 15

Megan

I'm heading into town to meet Betsy and the lawyer to sign the papers to take final ownership of the shop. I'm so excited I couldn't sleep last night. Every time I woke Hunter up, he just smiled and gave me orgasm after orgasm until I fell asleep again.

Since we've been home from Arizona for a week now, we've been staying in my bed together, and his stuff slowly makes its way into my room little by little. I give in today and tell him while I'm at the shop to just move his clothes to my closet, and we'll figure the rest out later.

The look on his face is so happy and full of love and joy. I make a silent promise to put that look on his face as often as possible.

Hunter also has given me the charm for my bracelet that signifies our trip. It's one of the famous red rocks with a cactus. He also bought me one of a hot tub, saying we had some of our hottest moments around that hot tub. This charm is to remember our first time and our first 'I love yous.' I love the charm bracelet because only we know what each one means, and looking at it reminds me of the best moments of our relationship.

I pull into the shop parking lot and just sit to take it in. This is what I've been pushing for so long. It's been my sole focus and my dream. It's still my dream, and I'm beyond excited to be here, but it's not the most important thing in my life anymore. Hunter holds that spot now.

And I'm okay with that.

I get out of the car and walk into the shop. Everyone cheers and I can't wipe the smile off my face if I tried.

"Oh, sweet girl, I'm so proud of you," Betsy says in her Southern drawl. She rushes over to give me a huge hug. What she lacks in her five-foot two-inch frame, she makes up for in spunk and sass. She's small, but no one wants to cross her.

"Thanks, Betsy. It felt like this day would never get here."

"Oh pish. I'm sure you had enough to keep you busy. Come back to the office. The papers are all ready for you."

We get seated, and her lawyer goes over the paperwork. Betsy signs everything first, then he goes over it with me. It's everything we had talked about many times before. Dad has looked over it with me as well.

I notice Betsy texting on her phone while the lawyer talks to me, but I don't think too much about it.

When it comes to my turn to sign, I hesitate just a bit and of course, Betsy catches it.

"What's wrong, sweet girl?"

I give her a nervous smile. "Now that this day is here, I'm a bit nervous is all. It's a huge responsibility."

"Oh, you know I'm always a phone call away if you have questions or need help. I'm not turning my back on you!"

"I know." I take a deep breath and sign the papers.

"Well, it's all yours," the lawyer, whose name I can never remember so I just stopped trying, says. He stands and shakes my hand. "I'll have the final paperwork to both of you next week." He walks out of the office, leaving just Betsy and myself.

"I couldn't be happier for anyone else to take this place over. You've done amazing things with it in the last few years, and I know you'll continue to make it grow," she says and hugs me again. When she pulls away, she dabs at her eyes. "I knew I'd be crying today. It's why I wore waterproof mascara and eyeliner." She laughs.

She takes my hand. "Let's take a walk around your shop, Megan."

When we walk out of the office, the shop is filled with people all yelling congratulations. My whole family is there, and Hunter is standing in front with a bouquet of wildflowers. I can't hold back the tears anymore.

I run to his arms and let the tears fall. "I can't believe you're here."

"You didn't think I'd miss such a huge moment, did you? I'm so proud of you, Megs. You've been talking about owning this place since the day we met, and now we stand here, and you did it!"

He lets go of me, and my family swarms in with hugs, telling me how happy and proud they are. Many of our regulars are here as well.

"Okay everyone, I figure this whole journey needs to end the same way it started. Megan, get in the chair. I'm giving you a haircut," Betsy says and laughs.

As I climb in the chair, I think about the day I sat in this chair, which is now mine, talking to Betsy. She said her daughter had no interest in the salon, and she didn't know what to do. I told her I'd love to buy it but had no clue how I'd ever afford it. I was sixteen at the time.

She offered me a job cleaning that day, and I took it. Anything to start learning the business thinking maybe someday I'd have my own place. Within a few months of taking that job she had me making appointments and cashing people out. I did that all through high school and when I turned eighteen, she proposed the idea to give me the shop.

It took everything I had not to jump at the chance, but I went home and talked to my family that night. After dinner, Hunter and I went for a walk and ended up at the Ranch Church. We talked and made plans and came up with ideas for the shop for hours. The next day, he drove me to the shop, and Betsy and I shook hands. She helped me enroll in classes the next day.

That seems like it was just yesterday, and now here we are. Betsy gives my hair a trim, does a bit of a reshape on it, and styles it for me. When she's done, she hugs me and tells me to celebrate. She'll cover the shop for the day.

Hunter is waiting for me when I head out of the shop.

"Let's grab lunch at the café." He takes my hand, and we walk since it's only a block away. When we walk in Jo, the café owner, rushes over.

"Oh Megan, I heard. Congratulations! I'm so happy you're taking over the salon!" Jo says and hugs me. "Lunch is on me! Come on, you two. Got your favorite booth set up for you!"

"Jo, you're so sweet! I had an idea I want to run by you when you have time."

"Hit me with it."

"Well, I'm noticing many husbands sitting in my waiting area, waiting for their wives to get their hair done. Maybe we could hand them a coupon to come down here and have coffee or lunch."

"I'm liking it so far. Keep going," she says, and Hunter and I take our seats.

"Well, I notice when the husbands are there, the women are more in a rush. It's harder to upsell them. If we can get the husbands out of the building, they won't be as stressed, and we can get some more upsell and book more appointments. They hang out with you snacking and maybe eating what their wives won't let them..."

"I love the idea. Draw up a proposal, and we can have a meeting sometime next week. Just text me, and we can work out a time."

I smile. "Will do." When I look back at Hunter, he has a huge smile on his face, shaking his head.

"What?" I ask.

"Look at you, power businesswoman. It's sexy as hell, Megan," he says and reaches across the table to take my hand. "Before we get interrupted again, I have a gift for you."

"Hunter..."

"I told you I would always spoil you, Megan. Someday, you'll stop fighting me on it," he says as he hands me a small box that looks like the one my charm for our trip came in. I'm right. When I open it, I find a charm with scissors, a comb, and lipstick. He takes the charm and adds it to my bracelet that I haven't taken off since our trip.

"I love it, Hunter."

"I figured this day deserves to be remembered on our timeline."

We don't get to talk too much more at lunch since everyone who comes in has heard the news. They stop by to congratulate me and talk for a few moments. The joys of a small town, and I wouldn't have it any other way. On the flip side, I get three appointments made from all the chatter.

Chapter 16

Hunter

Megan has been putting in some long hours at the shop, going over the books, and putting a game plan into place. When she gets home, I love that she crawls into bed with me and tells me everything. Hearing about her day and her ideas is the life I've always wanted.

It's what I saw growing up with my Mom and Dad. They love each other and share everything together. That's what I want with my wife, with Megan.

Now that we're done with dinner, I want to snag her away for a bit and go for a walk. I find her in the kitchen, helping Sage and Riley with dishes. Thankfully, they look almost done. I walk up behind Megan and place my arms around her waist.

"Want to go for a walk?" I ask and kiss her neck just below her ear.

She looks at me and smiles. "Yeah, give me just a minute, and I'll meet you by the barn?"

"Sounds good." I let go of her and head out the kitchen door towards the barn and take in the ranch. Next to the house is a line of pickup trucks. Everyone has a truck. Blaze even bought one for Riley recently. Then next to the barn, there are a few ranch trucks that get beat up running around the ranch.

Leaving the kitchen side door, the barn in front of me, and to the right is the driveway that takes me down to the main gate and out to the road. To the left is the driveaway that goes back to the bunkhouse and further on to some of the small cabins used for families on the ranch.

If you know where to look to the right of the barn is a path through the trees that leads you over to their parent's house. This is a path Blaze and Sage used all the time and it's still used by the family today.

I'm so lost in thought I don't hear Megan come up behind me. "Looks like you have a lot on your mind."

"Oh no, I was just taking in the ranch. It's been a while since I just took it all in."

She smiles at me, and I take her hand in mine.

THE COWBOY AND HIS OBSESSION

"Where to, cowboy?" she asks. I lead her down to the path that will take us out by her parents' house.

"Guess who came into the shop today."

"Who?"

"Cindy!"

"Did you two have fun catching up?"

"No!"

Uh oh, they used to be good friends but drifted apart about the time Cindy ditched her, and she met me. When Cindy went all boy crazy in high school, she also went all mean girl. Megan's words.

"She walked in demanding a walk-in appointment, which we don't have right now because I still have a chair I need to fill. Anyway, she was all, 'Oh I'll wait.' Well. I decided to skip my lunch and get her in, and she was all pissed because she had to wait an hour. I told her she needs an appointment and that we are booked with no walk-in slots currently."

"Have you thought about finding anyone to fill that chair?" I ask. I know she has mentioned it a few times before.

"That's not the point, Hunter."

Oh shit. She hasn't snapped at me like this in months. When she does, it's normally something big. I know from experience, she needs to get it out. I squeeze her hand to let her know she can keep talking.

"After she tried to tell me how to run my shop, she asks what kind of discount I plan to give her. I was shocked, so I asked her why she thought she was getting a discount. You ready for this?"

I don't think I am. "Ready."

"She said she's the whole reason you and I are together, and I should be down on my knees thanking her for ditching me that day, so I could meet you. No joke, she said that. Then it was like something out of a movie. The whole shop went dead quiet. The girls even turned off their hair driers. Want to know what I said to her?"

"Of course, baby," I say in a soft tone, so I don't escalate the situation even more.

"I said thank you for being a shitty friend and ditching me, so I could meet the love of my life. Thank you for being an even bigger shitty person now, and the only way you aren't paying full price is if I add on a 20% service fee for having to deal with your ass."

My jaw drops. Literally drops.

"Please tell me one of the ladies got all this on video."

"It's probably viral on Facebook by now."

"What did she say after that?"

"She said she was glad she ditched me and that she wasn't coming back to the shop. She would tell everyone she knew to stay away. I then charged her the extra twenty percent but didn't tell her. Of course, she didn't tip. Then on her way out, one of the girls yells, 'Hey Cindy, can you tell your people not to come to the shop sometime today. We need some more appointment slots opened up for the rest of us.' She got so mad, she stomped her foot and walked out."

By the end of her story, Megan is laughing, and I can't help but laugh too.

"Sounds like the little old ladies like you."

"Yeah, they do, and I love them to death too. They always have my back. But I need a game plan to find a new hairstylist. Even someone in school would help because they would have their nail license. That would open up a few free slots for the rest of us."

"Have you reached out to the local schools?"

"I have, but no one wants to move to such a tiny town. I interviewed one girl over the phone and when she found out we didn't even have a movie theater, she hung up on me."

"Ouch. What about putting up info at the high school for someone who wants to go to school? They can start like you did with cleaning and working the desk?"

She's silent for a bit. "That's a good idea. I'll get a few fliers made up and stop by the school to see if we can put them on the bulletin boards."

We round the corner and in front of us is the ranch church. Megan sees it and smiles.

"I love this place."

"Me too. Want to go inside for a bit?"

"Yes!" She does a little happy jump.

We walk in and take in the changes her dad and Blaze have made. Sage and Colt's wedding is in just a few weeks, and this place looks amazing.

"Oh, they finished the hardwood floors. Look how pretty they are!" she says.

"They do look great. The pews look good too with a good cleaning."

We sit in the back corner, same as always. I pull her on my lap.

"I can't wait to see a wedding here," she says, still looking around.

"You want to get married here?" I ask her.

"I always pictured my wedding here, so yeah."

I want to test the waters and see where her head is with us. How serious she is without scaring her off.

"I always loved it here too and pictured us getting married here."

Her eyes snap to mine and in them, I don't see an ounce of fear.

"You've thought of marrying me?"

I smile. "Yeah. About four years ago, I knew you were it for me. I knew I'd marry you. The question was just when."

She looks back toward the front of the church with a faraway look on her face.

"What do you think, baby? Can you see yourself marrying me someday?"

"Honestly, if you had asked me before our trip, it would have freaked me out. I'd have said it was moving way too fast. But sitting here with you today? Yeah, I can see it. I saw it when we walked in. I wasn't thinking of Sage and Colt's wedding."

My heart is beating so hard against my chest. She's finally on the same page as me. I want to drop down on one knee right now and ask her to marry me, to tell her I can't wait to be her husband, but my parents' words flash in my head. Take it slow.

So instead, I pull her closer in my arms and ask, "How were you picturing our wedding?"

She shifts closer to me and smiles, then rests her head on my shoulder.

"Twinkle lights strung from the rafters, making a lower ceiling. Candles everywhere, getting married at sunset by the light of the twinkle lights and candles. Of course, wildflowers like the ones in the field on the end of the pews. Maybe with mason jars. Burlap and lace bows. I like Sage's idea of couples standing across the altar instead of a bridesmaid side and groomsman side."

"I can picture it, and it's perfect. You know I can't wait to marry you, Megs. I promised we'd go slow, and we will but if it were up to me, we'd be married already."

"I know, Hunter, and you not rushing me means everything. I like how things are right now. But maybe after Sage and Colt have their day..." she trails off and shrugs her shoulder.

I kiss her temple and hug her close. We sit there for a while longer, just taking it all in. I'm picturing the wedding she talked about, and I plan to give it to her when she's ready, of course.

We make our way back to the house a little while later, just taking our time and enjoying the warm night breeze and each other's company.

Chapter 17

Megan

I'm spending the day in the shop today; I'm booked with appointments. I try Hunter's idea of posting fliers at the high school, and a week later, still nobody has reached out. Betsy says she had times like this too but to just wait it out. Someone will come in to fill the chair. It's always good to have a job opening in a small town.

I finish getting ready for work. It may be a hair salon, but I still like to wear my cowgirl style. Jeans and a gray-plaid button-down shirt and cowboy boots. I head downstairs and greet everyone. Sage has made blueberry muffins, so I grab one and fill my travel coffee mug as I eat.

I head out to my truck and set my coffee down when I see Hunter's truck coming up the drive. He left for a house call over an hour ago, so I didn't expect to see him this morning. I walk up to his truck and see he has the windows down, and his hair is slightly messed up from the wind. It looks so sexy.

He barely gets the door open before I get to the truck, so I lean in through the open window to give him a kiss. He wraps his hand around the back of my neck and pulls me as close as he can get me with the truck door between us.

I feel him smile on my lips and give my bottom lip a light bite. "I missed you," he whispers against my lips.

"I don't like you going to work early." I fake pout, which makes him smile. I back up from the truck, and he gets out.

"Colt called wanting me to check out a cow, and Sage asked me to check on a horse she just got in, so here I am."

"Well, I'm heading into the shop. Got a full day today."

"After this, I'm heading into the clinic for the day. Dad has a surgery he wants me there for, and I need some clinical hours over the summer."

"Okay, see you at dinner."

He leans in and gives me a soft slow kiss. "See you at dinner."

I head into town towards the shop and can't help but think how domestic that all is, and I love it. I want many more mornings like this and nights like a few nights ago at the church. The thought of getting married doesn't scare me. It never has. The thought of losing my best friend in the process is what scared me.

Hunter has been so patient and talking about marriage the other night doesn't scare me. It makes the butterflies come out in my belly. Like I can't wait to marry him.

Pulling into the shop, I'm the first one here like every morning. I go in the back, flip on the lights, and start my morning routine of turning everything on, making sure everything is stocked. I like this quiet time of the morning; it allows me to think.

About twenty minutes later, everyone comes in and sets up their stations, chatting. The doors open thirty minutes later. We're all booked solid again today.

An hour into our appointments, Joy Miller, who is the receptionist at the doctor's office in town, is in my chair for her cut and color when she asks about Sage's wedding.

"What can you tell us about Sage's wedding? We're all dying to know. You know she invited everyone. I heard even Kelli got an invite, though she has enough sense left not to go."

Kelli is Colt's ex. Well, they never dated, just slept together when Sage and he split. When Sage and Colt tried to work things out a few months back, Kelli tried to break them up. Kelli thought she and Colt were meant to be. I smile, thinking about how I helped Sage get her revenge on her with an early morning phone call service.

"Well, they're having it at the ranch church on the property."

"Oh, my word, there hasn't been a wedding there since your Mom and Daddy's wedding!" Mrs. Ida says. She was born and raised here in Rock Springs and has never left. She's also old enough to be my grandmother. "That wedding was so beautiful. I love that little church!"

"Yes, Blaze, Dad, and Colt have been working to fix it up. Some new paint, a good cleaning. They refinished the floors inside, and the windows on the sides all open. We think there'll be more people than pews, so some will have to stand outside."

"Who will be marrying them?" Ms. Ruby Lynn asks. Her husband passed away a few years back. They own a smaller ranch outside of town that her son now runs.

"Pastor Greg will and from what I understand, he's excited to be able to do so in the church. He's been asking Dad if he can do a special service there once a year to keep the history alive. I think Dad is going to agree now that it will be up and running."

Pastor Greg is from the church in town. He's younger, about my age, but everyone likes him. He's relatable and not afraid to get out in town and get his hands dirty helping people.

"What about the reception?" Mrs. Ida asks.

"It will be at the event barn like Blaze's was, but I guess she has plans to take it more outside. I'm not sure. She put Riley on reception duty. I'm in charge of hair, makeup, and nails obviously, and I've also been working on the decorations with them."

"Oh, I just can't wait. A wedding is always so much fun in Rock Springs!" Ms. Ruby Lynn says. "Will we be having another one to follow soon, Megan?" She raises an eyebrow at me.

"Now, Ms. Ruby Lynn, what's the first rule of gossip? You taught it to me the first day I walked into this shop."

She laughs. "Never talk about yourself."

"Exactly. Now if any of you know of a girl to fill that chair down there, please send her my way. Also, be on the lookout for a girl for Jason and Mac. Those two need to settle down!"

Everyone laughs.

I continue with my appointments—a lot of cuts and styles, more repeating of what I said earlier about Sage's wedding. We've been sending the husbands down to the café, and it's been working out great. Jo has also gotten into the habit of bringing up our lunches since we haven't been able to get out of the shop, and we've been sending her some good business.

Mrs. Willow is my after-lunch appointment, and she comes in about ten minutes early and rushes right in.

"Megan. Oh! Megan dear, I need to talk to you."

"Mrs. Willow, come sit in the chair. We can talk."

"Oh, Megan, I just got off the phone with my granddaughter. She left that no-good husband of hers. Remember they moved to Dallas when he took that job? Well, she walked in on him and his secretary going at it like rabbits! She's leaving him. Thank goodness they had no kids!"

"I'm so sorry to hear that, Mrs. Willow, though I know you never liked him," I say as I brush out her hair.

"No, I did not! Horrible two-faced man. Anyway, my Anna Mae called to ask if she could stay with me while she got on her feet. Of course, I said yes since we have so much extra room!"

"Oh, that's so sweet of you. I bet coming here will be just what she needs."

"She's excited. She loved spending summers here growing up, and I haven't seen much of her since she moved to Dallas."

"Give me a moment to mix your color for you, okay?"

"Okay, hurry up, dear. I haven't even gotten to the best part of the story!"

I laugh and head to the stock room to get the colors I need. I get them mixed up and head back to my chair.

"Okay, here we go, Mrs. Willow."

"Okay, so while Anna Mae was in Dallas, she took classes and got her nail and hair license and was working at a salon in Dallas there until yesterday."

I almost drop the brush I'm using to add color to her hair.

"Please tell me she wants a job," I say.

"Of course, child! That's what I've been trying to tell you! She'll be here tomorrow and soon as she gets settled in, I can send her up to talk to you. Now, this wouldn't be permeant; she has no intention of staying in Rock Springs right now, but I think it'll be a good six months. She wants to get the divorce finalized, get some money saved, and figure out her next steps."

I look to the side at the other girls who are looking at me. Some with their jaws dropped like me and huge smiles on their faces. If Anna Mae works out, that will be a huge stress reliever and more time off for us all. Even if it's just for now, it will give us plenty of time to find someone more permanent.

"Okay, who's offering their hair up for us to test her on?" I ask.

"Oh, I'm due for a cut and could use a new color," Jill volunteers.

"Perfect."

Mrs. Willow has a huge smile on her face that I'm sure matches my own. Finally, a bit of a break we've been hoping for. This is how the small-town grapevine can work for you as much as it can work against you.

Chapter 18

Megan

My last appointment at the shop was canceled, so I ask Jill to close. I want to surprise Hunter at the clinic and tell him about Anna Mae. I'm so excited. The buzz is all different at the shop after Mrs. Willow comes in and gives us the news. You can just see everyone has an extra bounce in their step.

I'm pulling into the animal clinic and parking on the side near Hunter's truck, so as to not take up spots up front. Before I can even get out of the car, my phone rings. It isn't a number I know, but running a business, I never ignore my phone.

"Hello?"

"Hello, is this Megan?" a woman asks.

"Yes, how can I help you?"

"Hi, my name is Anna Mae. grandmother told me you own the salon."

"Yes, she told me about you. I wasn't expecting to hear from you so soon."

"Oh, I'm sorry. I'm used to Dallas; spots don't stay open long. I didn't want to wait."

"Oh, I understand. We move a lot slower here in Rock Springs. Can you tell me where you went to school and the qualifications you have?"

She goes on to tell me about the school she went to in Dallas. It's a good one. She also took some extra coloring classes via the salon she worked at. As she's talking, I pull up the salon's Instagram page and see some of the hair she has done, and we talk a bit about that.

"Now, this isn't Dallas. I can't promise you'll make what you did there."

"Oh, I understand that. I just need to get back on my feet. Gramma isn't charging me rent, so I'll be able to build my savings."

"Good, now do you do nails too?"

"Oh, yes. I have some photos of some recent ones. The ladies in Dallas get all crazy with designs they want."

"Okay, well, we've been shorthanded for a while, so you'll be busy. We'll start you off on nails to free up time, and you'll take any walk-ins until the ladies get used to you. What I found works in the past is if each day you can get in a little early, we'll have you do one of the girls' hair to show off for the day. After that, a few walk-ins, and offer an intro price for appointments with you, word will spread fast."

We go on to talk about chair rent, employee rules, and tasks around the shop.

"Megan, it all sounds perfect."

"Oh well, the last thing I need is for you to come in and do a test. My assistant manager Jill offered. She needs a new color and cut. If all the girls agree and love it, then you have the job."

"Oh, thank you, Megan! When do you want me to come in?"

"Mrs. Willow said you're moving in tomorrow, so anytime after you get settled. Either after hours or over lunch break is best with how busy we are right now.

We set up a time for tomorrow. When we get off the phone, I have a huge smile on my face. Today is looking up!

I head into the clinic, but there's no one in the waiting room or at the desk. I hear voices in one of the exam rooms and since the door is open, I make my way down the hall. I stop short when I realize Hunter and his dad are talking about me.

"You serious about Megan?"

"Yeah, Dad, I am. I told you guys that at dinner a few weeks ago."

"I know, son. You just haven't dated at all, and it worries me."

"Why does that worry you, Dad?"

"Well, how do you know Megan's the one if you haven't seen what's out there?"

What? I always thought Hunter's parents liked me. I've been to his house many times, and they've said I'm like a daughter to them. They're so happy Hunter has a friend like me.

Maybe that's it. They're okay with Hunter being friends with me, but dating me is a whole other ball game. I just don't understand why I'm not good enough to date their son.

"Maybe you and Megan need to take a break. You're moving fast. Date around, make sure you still think she's the one," his dad says.

Date around? The thought of Hunter out with another girl makes me sick. I wouldn't be able to watch it. Worse if he broke up with me, saying he would date around; it would kill me. I know I wouldn't be able to go back to being his best friend, no matter how hard I tried. Hearing him talk about other girls would crush me.

"Where is this coming from Dad?"

That's not a no. Oh God, is he considering this? Would he do it? I don't think he would, but why not just shut it down? I know he's close to his parents. Would he do this to make them happy?

"I'm just worried you don't have the dating experience to see Megan's flaws is all. The more you date, the more you learn what you want."

Hunter doesn't answer right away. Oh God, I can't listen to this anymore. With tears in my eyes, I head back to the front and slip out to my truck as quietly as possible, and just cry.

· · · ● · ● ● · · ·

Hunter

I pause and take a deep breath before I say something I can't take back. I look my father in the eyes before answering him.

"Megan's flaws? Dad, I've spent every day for the last eight years with her. I know her flaws, and she knows mine. I know her better than anyone. It took me years to get her to give me a chance, why would I mess with that? I don't need to date around to know I'm head over heels in love with her. She's the air that I breathe. The thought of another woman touching me makes me sick. There's no way I could date anyone else. I have absolutely no doubt she's the one. Any doubt you and Mom have is irrelevant."

Dad's face hasn't changed as I talk, and I wonder if he's hearing me. Every second of silence, and my anger tips up another notch. Suddenly, his face bursts into a huge smile, and for the first time in my life, I want to sucker-punch my father.

"That's what I wanted to hear."

"What?" I'm completely confused.

"You've been so hesitant to tell us your true feelings, I was worried you weren't sure of how you felt. I needed to be sure. Megan is so amazing. She deserves the world, and I couldn't stand to see you hurt her because you weren't sure."

"Dad, you could have just asked. I was a minute from punching you in the face."

Dad laughs. "Dad did the same thing to me when I was talking about your mom being the one. I remember the feeling well."

I run my hand through my hair and then shake my head.

"I'm going home," I say, still not happy. Right now, I just need to hold my girl.

Dad chuckles. "I got this. Go to your girl and bring her for dinner next week."

"Okay, tell Mom I love her."

I head out to my truck, shaking my head. When I round the corner, I see Megan's truck in the parking lot and her head bent over the wheel. My heart races, is she okay?

I'm halfway to her truck when she looks up. That's when I can tell she has been crying. My heart stops, then races again. It feels like it's being torn out of my chest. I'll kill anyone who has hurt my girl. I pick up the pace to get to her truck, but her eyes go wide. She backs out of her spot and leaves the parking lot.

What the hell? Is she running from me? I take off to my truck and get in. As I pull out of the parking lot, I wait for my phone to connect to Bluetooth, trying to call her. She doesn't pick up. The second time, it goes straight to voicemail.

"Fuck!" I scream into my truck and hit the wheel. I'm going to assume she was heading back to the ranch, so that's where I head.

What has her so upset she's running from me? Then a thought crosses my mind. Could she have walked in and heard the middle of Dad's conversation? It was enough to make me mad, but she only heard part of it... I don't want to assume anything until I know.

I pull into the ranch and thank God her truck is there. I barely get my truck shut off, and I'm flying up the steps into the kitchen. I scan the kitchen and dining room looking for her. I don't find her, but I do find Blaze and Colt blocking my way upstairs. Sage is to my left in the kitchen, glaring at me.

"What did you do to her?" Blaze asks.

"I didn't do anything. I came out of the clinic and saw her crying in her truck. She took off before I could even get to her."

"What were you doing at the clinic?" Sage asks.

"I was talking to Dad."

"About what?" Mac sounds annoyed.

I run my hand down my face. "Dad was trying to convince me to date other people when I finally snapped at him. I told him how I felt about Megan. He smiled and said he was waiting for me to say exactly how I felt. I wanted to punch him for the first time in my life."

They all look at each other. "Did you talk to her at all today?" Sage asks.

"No, I saw her when she left for work, and I had just pulled in to look at that cow you asked me to, Colt. I haven't talked to her since then. We were both busy today."

Everyone looks at me but doesn't say a word, then looks at Sage.

"Maybe I should talk to her," Sage sighs.

"No." I take a step toward the stairs, but Blaze and Colt don't move. "I'm going up even if I have to fight my way through both of you. That's my girl up there, and something upset her. You can't keep me away."

Blaze and Colt look at each other and then step aside. I waste no time. I run up the stairs two at a time. When I get to her room, I try the door handle and find it locked.

I knock. "Megan baby, open up," I say softly.

I hear a muffled, "Go away," from the other side, and I can tell she's still crying.

"Baby, open up so we can talk. I can't fix it if you don't tell me what's wrong."

"You can't fix this, Hunter; just go away."

Fuck. I need to get in there. The bathroom!

I run into my room and through the bathroom to find she locked her bathroom door too. Damn it.

I look for a paperclip in my room and head back out into the hallway. When I start messing with her door, she must have heard me because she flings the door open and sighs.

"Really, Hunter?"

"Yes, really," I say and stalk towards her, forcing her to back up. Once inside her room, I close the door. I go to wrap my arms around her, but she pulls back.

"Megan baby, you got to tell me why you're crying."

She won't look at me, and she isn't talking. She doesn't want me touching her either.

"Megan," I beg.

She meets my eyes, and I see her square her shoulders. Oh, that's a signature Megan move that I'm not going to like what comes next.

"I think we should break up," she says and in one sentence not just my heart shatters but my whole world. I feel tears at the back of my eyes, and my whole world is thrown upside down. I have to put my head on the wall to hold myself up.

"Talk to me please. Tell me what happened." I have to know what happened if I'm going to have a chance in hell to fight it.

When she still doesn't speak, I try again. Saying words that betray every fiber of my being.

"If you want to break up, you have to tell me why. I deserve that at least. Tell me the truth, and I'll walk out that door right now."

I watch her eyes well up. "I heard your dad at the clinic today. I can't be the reason your family breaks up. I know how close you all are."

"You didn't stay to hear the end, did you?"

"No, and it doesn't matter. Let's just end this while we can still go back to being friends. Just go, Hunter." She shakes her head and crosses her arms.

I'm staring at her in disbelief. It takes everything in me to walk out of that room, but I know she needs space. Every step I take away from her kills me. Before I step into the hallway, I stop.

"I'm not going anywhere, Megan. I think this is just a cop-out for being scared. I'll give you a few days, but I'm not backing down." I close the door behind me and walk back downstairs.

Before I even hit the stairs, the tears I had tried to stop run down my face. I skip the kitchen, not wanting to talk to anyone. They see me anyway and call out, trying to get my attention. I walk out the front door and collapse on the front steps.

I don't even think as I pull out my phone and call Dad.

"Hey, son."

"She broke up with me because she heard your asinine conversation at the clinic. She didn't hear the end, but she doesn't want to break up the family, so she broke up with me."

"I'm sorry. I never would have said anything if I knew she was there."

"Yeah, a lot of good it does me now. You can explain to Mom why I won't be at family dinner until this gets fixed," I say and then hang up. I've never hung up on Mom or Dad before, and I've never skipped family dinner. Hell, I've never talked to Dad like that either.

I set my phone down, cross my arms over my knees, and bring my head down and not knowing what else to do I just cry.

Chapter 19

Megan

After Hunter walks out of my room, I go back to my bed and cry. I don't even go down for dinner. An hour later, Sage comes up with a plate of food for me. Even if you're sick, you have to eat something. Family rule.

"You need to at least eat something. Blaze and Colt are threatening to come up and force feed you," she says.

I don't even smile. I just sit up and pick at the pork chops she brought up.

I know Sage is waiting for me to tell her what happened. I also know she has no plans of leaving until I do. I take a few minutes to gather my thoughts.

"We broke up."

"I gathered that by watching him cry, walking out the front door."

Then she waits again. Sage is good at waiting until you tell her what she wants to know.

When we were in high school, she thought Hunter and I were having sex, so she waited me out an hour until I admitted I was a virgin and offered to go to the doctor to prove it.

"I think I found a girl to fill the chair at the salon. I was so excited, so when my last appointment canceled, I went to the clinic, thinking I'd surprise Hunter. I go in, and I hear his dad telling Hunter he should break up with me and date other girls because he hasn't dated enough and doesn't know my flaws."

Sage looks at me like she's just been slapped. "That doesn't make sense. His parents are good friends with Mom and Dad, and I know they love you."

"I thought so too. You know how close his family is. I can't be what tears them apart. Plus, the thought of Hunter dating someone else makes me sick. I came straight here and can't seem to stop crying."

Sage puts the plate of food on my end table, crawls into bed with me, and pulls me into her arms.

"Well, I'm here as long as you need me. Let it all out."

I eventually fall asleep when I can't cry any more tears.

• • • ● • ● • • •

I wake up the next morning and don't even bother trying to hide how shitty I feel. Jeans and a t-shirt and my hair tossed up in a messy bun. If I didn't have a full schedule today, I wouldn't even be going in. I step into the kitchen, and there's Hunter.

He doesn't look like he slept a wink. His eyes are red, and the dark circles under his eyes match mine. His hair is messed up like he's been running his hands through it. A move I love watching him do.

No, don't think about him like that.

His eyes lock on mine, pleading at me to take him back, to not let this be the end, but I can't.

I know everyone is watching from the dining room table, so I walk over and pour my to-go cup of coffee, and head to my truck.

As I near the salon, I try to give myself a pep talk and figure what I'll tell people. If they don't know yet, they'll know something is wrong. I guess I can blame it on being up late helping with Sage's wedding.

As the morning goes on, everyone seems to accept the excuse of me helping Sage, and I know my family will cover for me too.

About an hour before lunch, a young woman walks in with perfectly highlighted hair and manicured nails.

"Hi, I'm here to see Megan," she says to Jill, who happens to be at the desk.

"That would be me," I say.

"Oh, hello! I'm Anna Mae I wanted to come to introduce myself."

"Nice to meet you. Not my best day," I say, gesturing at myself.

"Oh, not to worry."

"Jill, do you have any lunch plans?"

"Yep, I plan to get my hair done."

"Well, Anna, this is Jill. Let's see what you got."

Anna has great energy and a vibe that I know she'll fit in with the girls here. By the time she's done, even I have to admit she's good. Too good for Rock Springs, Texas, but I'll keep her as long as I can.

"Well, looks like the chair is yours. Did you bring your paperwork with you?"

"Yes, let me run out to my car to get it."

"Okay, I need to run to the café and grab some lunch. I haven't eaten today. I'll be right back."

Jo can tell right away something is wrong with me but doesn't ask. She just adds a brownie to my lunch bag for me with a wink.

I walk back into the shop and see Hunter. He's talking to Anna Mae, and I can tell she's flirting. Hunter walks away mid-sentence when he sees me.

"I can't do this here, Hunter. I'm trying to work."

"You didn't tell me you found a girl for the chair."

"That's what I was coming to the clinic to tell you yesterday." I don't have to say anything more; he knows why I didn't get a chance to tell him.

"Have lunch with me," he begs. I hold up my lunch bag for the café.

"Megan," he sighs.

I smile over at Anna Mae. "Sorry, just give us a few minutes," I say to her then turn to Hunter. "Out back."

He follows me out the back door. The door barely closes, and I spin to face him, catching him off guard.

"This proves I was right," I say, and he looks at me, confused.

"About what?"

"I can't be around you and see other girls flirting with you, or run into you with someone else."

"Dammit, Megan. I don't want her, or anybody else. I don't want anyone but you. I. Want. You. Megan."

My eyes water again, dammit.

"Did we ruin this, Hunter? We can't even be friends now, can we?"

"Megan. I'm still your friend and will be here for you for anything. I'm so damn happy you found someone to fill that chair. I know you were stressed."

"It's not permanent. She's staying with her grandma, Mrs. Willow. She's getting a divorce, and she worked at a salon in Dallas."

Small talk, we can do small talk. My heart doesn't hurt so bad with small talk.

"When does she start?"

"I'm going over her paperwork and plan to talk to her about that now. She did a great job on Jill's hair."

He nods and hangs his head, looking at his feet.

"I'll let you get back in there. But I'm here, Megan, and I'm not going anywhere." I nod and walk around him. I put my hand on the door when he calls for me.

"Megan?"

I turn to look at him. "I love you." I close my eyes. I can't say it even though I do love him with all my heart. His words heal my soul and break my heart at the same time. I just nod and walk back inside.

Anna Mae starts the next day and fits right in. The girls coming in for appointments love her, and a few people walk in to check her out. Hunter stops by and brings me lunch.

"I want to make sure you're eating, Megs," he says. Before he turns to leave, he looks me in the eyes and says it again, "I love you, Megs."

Once he leaves, Anna comes up to me.

"I'm sorry. I didn't know he was yours. He was just being nice. It's been a while since a guy was nice to me is all. I'm sorry if I overstepped."

I nod but don't correct her. Even if he isn't mine anymore, I can't stomach the thought of the two of them together.

Chapter 20

Megan

Hunter stops by with lunch every day for a week, and every day he leaves with an, 'I love you.' At home, he's been giving me space. He still sits to eat dinner with us. Sage won't let either of us flake on that, and he watches and listens when I talk about the salon but stays quiet unless he's asked a direct question.

Every night, he sends the same text message, give or take a few words. Like the one he sent tonight.

Hunter: You're still it for me, Megs. I'm here waiting as long as you need. I love you with my whole heart and miss you. -Hunter

He knows how to slowly chip away at a girl's wall. Every night I read the text but don't answer. Some nights I fall asleep staring at the text, but tonight something feels different. I can't put my finger on it. Maybe it's just a part of the wall he has managed to chip away.

I feel like I can't *not* reply. So, that's what I do.

Me: I miss you too, Hunter.

Short and sweet. Once I hit send, I stare at my phone. A few minutes go by and nothing back. Did I shock him or is he not going to reply? A few more minutes and still nothing. I take a deep breath and as I'm about to set my phone down, he finally messages me back.

Hunter: I'm here, Megs. Get some sleep, beautiful. Good night.

My heart tries to leap out of my chest. Part of me wants to run to his room, climb into bed with him, and feel his arms around me. The other part frantically tries to rebuild the wall to protect me when he realizes losing his family over me isn't worth it.

I fall asleep with my phone in my hand, again.

The next day at the salon, I'm in the middle of Grace Murphey's color touch up when Hunter's dad walks into the salon. You could have knocked me down with a feather. When his eyes make contact with mine, he nods.

"I reckon it's time for a haircut if you can squeeze me in Megan."

"Sorry, I'm booked solid," I say, turning back to Grace's coloring, but I can still watch him in the mirror.

"That's okay. I'll sit here in case a spot opens up." He sits in the waiting area and picks up a beauty magazine, crosses one ankle over his knee, and proceeds to read it. I feel like this is the start of a bad joke. A cowboy in a beauty salon, reading a hair magazine...

I look back to the mirror, and Grace's eyes are wide as they look at me. It's gotten around town about Hunter's lunchtime rituals and how we barely talk. I'm sure people suspect we're fighting and not broken up.

Then Grace does something that shouldn't shock me, being in Rock Springs.

She says loudly, "Oh well, Anna Mae can finish my color. That opens Megan up for your cut, Hank."

I take a deep breath and nod. I help Grace over to Anna's chair and get her set up, then head back to my chair and clean up.

"Right this way, Mr. Norwood," I say with a hand out to my chair.

"I think we've known each other long enough that you can call me Hank."

"I don't think we know each other at all, Mr. Norwood." He looks hurt, and the shop quiets down quite a bit. "What kind of cut can I do for you today?"

"Just a trim and clean up the sideburns and the neck." I nod and get to work.

"I understand you heard the conversation I had with Hunter that day at the clinic."

"I did."

"I'm also guessing you didn't stick around to hear the end of it."

"No, didn't see the point, really."

"I wish you had," he says, and I stay silent. No point in saying anything because whatever he has to say, I'm not sure I want to hear it.

"See, Hunter is a lot like me. He loves fiercely, but sometimes he isn't good at expressing his feelings. Now his mom and I've known how he feels about you since you two were in high school, but we weren't sure if he knew how deeply he felt for you."

"So, you thought he should date other people and decided to be vocal about it. Got it."

The shop goes dead quiet; even the hair driers are silenced. There's no way anyone who's here will miss this prime Rock Springs gossip. I'm sure this is the exact reason most of the ladies are in here every week.

Hank chuckles. "Actually, I was pushing him to make him mad enough to admit to me how he feels about you." This catches my attention, and I stop what I'm doing to look at him in the mirror. "He did too. He went off on me in a way I've never seen him tell me off. How dare I even suggest a thing, and how you're the one. The air he breathes, and he even went as far as to say the thought of touching another woman makes him sick. He was so mad at me when I started laughing but finally, he admitted it."

"He may not have admitted it to you, but he has said all that to me and more daily since we've been together."

I see something close to regret on his face, then he nods.

"He called me later that night in tears. He's still mad at me. He won't talk to me unless it's about the clinic, and he won't come home to family dinners. My wife is even mad at me. So mad I've been eating TV dinners since that night."

There's a collective gasp in the room. In the South, if your woman is pissed off at you, she won't cook for you. She'll warm you up a TV dinner in the microwave, toss it down in front of you, and walk away. Well, that's how we do it here in Rock Springs anyway. It makes me feel better in a way. I continue with his hair, and he continues to speak.

"I know I deserve it. I went about it the wrong way, but it's what my Daddy did to me when I was serious about my wife. It worked and a week later, we were engaged. That's all I was pushing for with Hunter. We've always thought of you like family and honestly, if Hunter had agreed and said he was breaking up with you to date someone else, I'd have given him a good ole ass whooping with my belt right there in the middle of the clinic."

I give him a half-smile at that. Trying to picture him getting one up on Hunter long enough to give him a beating is a funny picture. Hunter is bigger than his dad and a bit faster.

I finish his hair and hand him the mirror.

"You always do an amazing job, Megan. I hope you both figure this out, and I see you and my son for dinner soon. I'm not sure what's holding you back, but I wanted you to know the full story, and I wanted to apologize for the role I played in this. That wasn't my intention in any way. I think you two are perfect for each other, and my wife keeps telling me to fix this because she needs grandbabies."

He pays and tips twenty dollars on a bill less than that. Then he tips his hat and heads out. The door closes, and the shop slowly buzzes back to life. I barely make it back to my office before I burst into tears. I don't have any more appointments until after lunch, so I try to get some bookkeeping done, but my thoughts keep going back to what Hunter's dad said.

It seems my breaking up with Hunter has done exactly what I didn't want to happen. I didn't want to drive him and his parents apart, but he isn't even talking to them. There's a light knock on my door.

"Hunter's here," Jill says.

I stand and check my makeup and hair before heading out. I decide to extend an olive branch. I'm not ready to jump back into a relationship, but I do know I want my best friend back. He's been right there in the wings, waiting for me. It's time to take a step.

He looks at me with a sad smile. I know he can tell something is wrong but doesn't think we're at a point where he can ask. He holds up lunch, and I smile at him.

"Do you have time to eat with me?" I ask and watch as surprise crosses his face before he nods.

I head out the back door to my truck in the parking lot and pull the tailgate down. I hop up then look back at Hunter. I can tell it's hard for him to keep his hands to himself. He's so used to always being near me and close to me. He normally would have helped me on to the tailgate without even thinking about it. Even before we started dating.

I smile at him as he sits next to me.

"Did you eat already?" I ask.

"Yeah," he says. I nod and pull out the BLT sandwich from the café, no tomato of course, and take a bite.

We just sit there in silence for a few minutes before I say, "So, your dad came in to get a haircut today. Grace gave up her spot and had Anna Mae finish her color just so I could give him his haircut."

Hunter looks over at me. I can tell he's studying me, but I stare straight ahead at the salon's back door.

"He told me about the full conversation and apologized. Told me you haven't been home for family dinner. He's been eating TV dinners every night since. Your mom is pissed."

Hunter lets out a sarcastic laugh. "Yeah, I don't see the point of going over for dinner just to sit there and stare at each other in silence or fight."

"Have you talked to your mom at least?"

"No, you know how she is, a true Southern lady. She backs her husband up even if she doesn't agree."

I nod. I've seen it countless times with Mom and Dad. Dad will say or do something, and Mom is sweet as pie until they get home, and she goes off. Yelling, slamming doors. Once, she threw a loaf of bread at Dad.

"Remember that time Dad made a few jokes about Mom's cooking at the Cattleman's Association Gala? The moment we all got back to the house, she went off." I ask.

"Oh my God, yes. That was when she threatened to put locks on the pantry and the fridge so he couldn't touch her food."

"Yes, she wouldn't even make his TV dinners. All he was allowed was toast because that's what Mom thought they got in prison."

"Yes! That was the time she threw the loaf of bread at him."

"Yep, she did it in front of you. That was the moment we knew you were part of the family when she didn't wait for you to go home."

He sobers back up and nods but stares straight ahead. I bump my shoulder into his.

"You're still family, and we'll get through this. I got the full story, but I still need time."

"I'll be here waiting. Take all the time you need, Megan."

I smile at him. "I'm still here if you need me to. You're still my best friend."

"And the same goes for me. I'll always be here for you, Megs."

"Maybe tomorrow you bring your lunch and eat with me?" I ask as I take another bite of my sandwich.

He smiles. "I'll be here."

Chapter 21

Hunter

I walk out of the beauty shop with a smile on my face. Today we've made progress. Megan had lunch with me, and we talked. I have more hope and more fight in me now.

When I got the reply text message from her last night, I sent up a silent prayer that it was the start of repairing us. It took everything in me not to shout for joy when she asked me to sit with her over lunch.

I'm shocked to hear that Dad came to talk to her but glad he did. It still doesn't make things okay with him and me, and it won't until Megan is mine again. Then he and I can work it out.

Late at night on the days following our breakup, I had to think, what if I couldn't win her back? What if this was it for good? Could I forgive Dad? Then I didn't think so but now I don't think I'd really have a choice to but I'm not ready to yet.

I made myself a promise that first night to not give up. I was still taken as far as I was concerned, and I'd still treat her like she was mine. That's why I bring her lunch every day and make it a point to tell her I love her. I want to make sure I tell her every day.

I decide to text her every night before bed too. I want her to know she's on my mind. I want to know that if this doesn't work out, I've done everything I possibly can. I don't want to look back thinking I lost the love of my life because I didn't do this or that.

The rest of the day goes by in a blur of house calls. A snake bite to a dog, a check-up at the stables, and a few vaccinations. By the time I'm heading home, I'm tired but excited to see Megan and what the night holds. For the first time in a while, I'm hopeful about going home.

Hopeful I can steal a few minutes with Megan. Hopeful we'll talk. Hopeful I'll get to hold her in my arms soon.

I walk into the house and find Megan helping Sage with dinner. When Megan sees me, she gives me a soft smile that makes my heart skip a beat. It's been way too long since she has smiled at me.

"Can I help you ladies with anything?" I ask.

Sage smiles at me and says, "Why don't you set the table. We'll be ready in about ten minutes."

I move around the kitchen, getting plates, cups, and silverware to set on the table. Everyone piles in for dinner, gathering around the tabletop in the kitchen, and the house comes to life. I love this time of day when we all get together for dinner, no matter what we're doing.

We sit for dinner, and I listen to Megan talk about how everyone seems to be taking to Anna Mae and how she finally has a few regulars. I feel my phone go off in my pocket. I don't like checking my phone at the table. For the most part, we have a no-phone rule, but it could be an emergency call, so I always check it.

This time I see it's my Dad, so I send him to voicemail and focus back on Megan. I notice she stops talking and checks her phone, then gives me a funny look, and answers it, "Hello?"

She's quiet for a few minutes then I see her face pale.

"Yeah, he's right here. Hang on." Then she turns to me. "Hunter, it's about your mom," she says softly and hands me the phone.

"Hello?"

"Son, your mom's been in a car accident. They're taking her to the hospital now. I'm on my way there. I'll let you know when I know something."

Fuck.

"Dad, I'm on my way. See you there." I stand and hand Megan her phone back. "Mom was in a car accident. My dad is on his way to the hospital. He doesn't know anything."

Megan stands. "Come on, I'll go with you."

"Call us and let us know what's going on and what you need. We can be there if you need us. We can reschedule appointments at the clinic, make food, bring clothes. Whatever, just let us know," Sage says.

"Thanks." My mind races. Megan knows this and takes my hand.

"Come on, Hunter. I'll drive," she says softly, and we head out to her truck.

The whole way there I'm sending up silent prayers that Mom will be okay and kicking myself for not going to dinner this week. As if reading my mind, Megan reaches over and takes my hand. She doesn't offer false words of hope; she just squeezes my hand, offering me comfort.

When we pull up to the hospital and get into the ER waiting room, I see Dad pacing the waiting room. I rush up and hug him.

"Any word?" I ask.

"She was hit by some teen who was texting and not paying attention. They ran a red light and hit the passenger's side, and the car flipped a few times. She was unconscious when the paramedics got on the scene, so they're assessing her injuries now."

I nod and feel Megan's hand rubbing my back.

"She's too stubborn to not be okay," I say, and that makes Dad smile for just a second.

"I'm glad you're here, son," Dad says quietly and then hugs me.

"We're family, Dad. No matter what happens."

When he pulls away, I think I see a glimmer of tears in his eyes, but he turns away and paces the waiting room again.

Megan wraps an arm around my waist. "You need anything? Coffee, cupcakes, whiskey?"

"No, just you." I turn and pull her into a hug.

"You have me, Hunter. Always have, always will. I'm not going anywhere," she whispers.

Then a doctor comes out. "Family of Donna Norwood?"

"That's us. I'm her husband," Dad says.

"She's unconscious but stable. They had to cut her from the car. She has a lot of bruises and a bump on her head, a broken arm, and a deep cut on her leg. We ran some scans, and there's no internal bleeding, and her head looks good. She has a few stitches in the cut on her leg. It looks like it was from some glass. She's going to be fitted for a cast now. We expect her to wake up anytime. This is just her body's way of dealing with the pain."

"When can we see her?" Dad asks.

"Well, she's being moved to a room now. Soon as she's set up, I'll send a nurse down to get you."

"Thank you, Doctor," Dad says and shakes his hand, and I do the same.

Megan takes my hand. "Come sit," she says softly and pulls me toward the chairs. I sit with her, but she doesn't let go of my hand.

About twenty minutes later, a nurse comes out. "Family for Donna Norwood."

We all stand, and I drag Megan with me. No way am I going in there without her.

"I'm her husband, this is my son, and my daughter-in-law," Dad says without missing a beat. The nurse nods.

"Follow me."

I squeeze Megan's hand, and we all follow the nurse up to Mom's room.

"She's in here. We aren't busy, so she should have her own room for the time being. Be careful of her tubes; it's just an IV and some monitors. Talk to her, many say it helps. Press the nurse button when she wakes up or if you need anything," the nurse says before leaving us at the door.

We follow Dad in, and we all stand at the foot of Mom's bed. She has some bruises on her face and a cut above her eyebrow, and the cast is visible. Otherwise, she looks like she's asleep and just a bit pale. Dad takes the recliner by the bed, and Megan and I stay where we are.

"Thank you, Dad, for getting Megan back here," I say.

He waves me off. "She's family, always has been. You two just need time to sort it out and make it happen. Give us grandbabies."

I groan. "Not you too."

"I have to since your mom can't right now." Then he looks over at Mom. "Donna, baby, Hunter is here with Megan too. You need to wake up for us. I need to see those brown eyes of yours."

I smile. The love my parents show each other is what I want. I take Megan's hand and walk to the chair on the other side of the bed.

"Sit down, Megs," I say.

"I'm fine. You sit," she says, and I shake my head, sit, and grab her around the waist to pull her onto my lap.

"Problem solved," I say. She doesn't say anything, just wraps her arms around my shoulders. We sit and talk about anything and everything over the next hour.

When Megan talks about Anna Mae's suggestions of painting the inside of the shop bright neon colors, Mom stirs. After a minute, she opens her eyes and makes eye contact with Dad, then me then Megan.

Of course, her first words are, "Don't you dare go painting that shop neon colors! It will give us all headaches!"

Which makes us all laugh. The nurses come in, followed by the doctor. They plan to keep her for monitoring for a few days before they send her home.

We stay for a bit and talk. Mom may be in a hospital bed, but she hasn't lost any of her sass.

"You two work it out yet, so we can start having family dinners again?" she asks Dad.

"Yes, Mom. I'll be over for dinner and even cook it myself the night you get home."

"Good. What about you and this sweet girl? I need grandbabies, you know," Mom says, referring to Megan. I'm not quite sure what to say, but Megan beats me to it.

"Hank came in and talked to me today. He told me the whole story. Hunter and I are working on it, I promise."

I squeeze her hip as a thank you.

"You'll be at the next family dinner, you hear me?" Mom says, and Megan laughs.

"Of course, Donna. I wouldn't miss it."

I notice it's close to eleven p.m., and I know Megan has work in the morning as do I.

"Dad, are you staying here?" I ask, already knowing the answer.

"Yes. I don't leave until she does."

"Okay. I'll head into the clinic tomorrow and reschedule the next few days of appointments for you. I'll pack a bag for both of you and bring it with me tomorrow. Let me know if you need anything else."

"Yes, call or text. Sage and Riley are ready to help. I know they'll be stocking your freezer."

Dad smiles. "Will do, thank you. Hunter, text me when you get home, so I know y'all made it safe, okay?"

"Promise, Dad."

The drive home is a lot more like being in the car with Megan used to be. We're talking, and it's just an easygoing vibe.

"So, I'm going to call Jill when we get home and have her open tomorrow. I'll go into the clinic with you to help reschedule appointments for the week."

"You don't need to do that. I know you're booked."

"Hunter, Anna Mae needs clients anyway, and there's no one tomorrow who doesn't know about your mom already or will be surprised I'm not there. One day to help you reschedule a week of appointments isn't a big deal. You won't talk me out of it."

"Stubborn girl." I shake my head. "Thank you, Megs."

She squeezes my hand and holds it the rest of the way home.

Chapter 22

Megan

I lie in bed thinking about the events of tonight. Hunter stays downstairs when we get home to fill everyone in. I come upstairs to call Jill and get ready for bed. Jill says she had planned to come in and open anyway soon as she heard about Hunter's mom. She agrees to move clients over to Anna Mae and take on whoever won't go to her.

I love the girls at my shop. Now I'm lying in bed waiting for Hunter's good night text, wondering if I'll get one tonight or not with everything going on. I wouldn't blame him one bit if I didn't get one tonight; he has a lot on his mind.

I'm starting to drift off when I hear the bathroom door open. I open my eyes to see Hunter standing next to my bed, looking sexy as hell and a little unsure.

I sit up. "Everything okay?" I ask and watch him run his hand through his hair.

"Yeah, it's just..." He sighs. "Can I hold you, Megan? I need my best friend tonight."

I don't even hesitate. I scoot over to the middle of the bed and pat the spot I was just lying in. He climbs into bed and pulls the covers up over us. I turn over and feel him press his chest up to my back. He scoots one arm under my pillow, and his other arm goes around my waist and pulls me as close to him as he can get me.

He buries his face in my hair and just breathes me in for a few minutes.

"Thank You, Megan, for today and for this. I love you."

I can't hold it back this time, and I don't want to.

"I love you too, Hunter. I have a feeling we'll be fine."

"I hope so. I don't think I can live without you in my life."

I don't know what to say. So, I just rub his arm and say good night. The last thing I remember... he's still awake as I drift off to sleep.

• • • ● ●• ● •• •

The next morning, he isn't in bed when I wake up. I take a moment to register that I'm disappointed. I miss waking up with him and had hoped to get the chance to this morning. I get ready, head downstairs, and find him sitting at the dining room table with his phone.

"Hey, I was thinking we could take my truck since we're going to the same place this morning," he says while I make my coffee.

"I was thinking I'd follow you over. I need to swing by the shop on the way home."

"I can take you. It's not a problem."

"Well, if you don't mind then riding with you sounds good."

I sit at the table and eat a quick breakfast before heading to the clinic. Once there, I pull up the appointments.

"Why don't you work on rescheduling your house calls, and I'll start on today's appointments."

"Okay, I'll be in my office if you need me."

Making phone calls, I discover everyone has already heard about Hunter's mom and is happy to move their appointments around. They ask how she's doing and if Hunter and Hank need anything. By lunchtime, I have all that day's appointments rescheduled, about to start on the following day when there's a knock on the door.

I get up and see Anna Mae outside, so I let her in.

"Everything okay at the shop?"

"Oh, yes. The girls and I figured you wouldn't get out to eat so I volunteered to bring you two some food. I just told Jo who it was for, she made it, and I have no clue what it is."

"Thanks, I plan to stop by when we're done. I'm helping him reschedule appointments right now."

"Yeah, we heard. Let us know if you need anything, okay?"

"Thanks, girl." I give her a quick hug and lock the door behind her.

I walk back to Hunter's office as he's wrapping up a phone call. I hold up the bag from the café.

"The girls at the shop sent lunch."

"Good, I'm starving." I spread out the contents of the bag across his desk, and it's all our favorites.

"I wrapped up all the house calls. Where do you want me to start on the clinic schedule?"

"I got all of today's appointments rescheduled. Why don't you work on tomorrow's, and I'll move Monday's around?"

"Perfect." We talk about some of the weird questions we got while moving appointments and just laugh like old times.

Once we finish eating, we get back to work. I reschedule Monday and Tuesday's appointments in the time it takes him to do Fridays. I knew everyone would want to talk to him. I figure if they need more time, I can come in on Monday and do some more rescheduling for them.

I wrap up and head into Hunter's office. He's on the phone, so I stand in the doorway and take him in. He loves this clinic and the clients, so he takes his time and answers their questions, not just on their pets but on his mom and dad. It's what makes him an amazing vet—he cares.

When he looks up and sees me, he smiles and wraps up the phone call.

"I have one more to reschedule."

"I got Monday and Tuesday's done. If you still need more time, I'll come back Monday and reschedule the rest of the week."

"Thank you. This has been such a huge help."

"Of course, Hunter. Now get going on that last appointment." He dials and starts talking when they pick up.

I walk over to him and place my hand on his shoulder. He looks up at me, and I go to sit on his lap. When I was on his lap last night in the hospital room, I realized just how much I missed this kind of closeness with him and how much I missed him.

He wraps an arm around my waist and continues his phone call without missing a beat. He reschedules, gets off the phone, and wraps his arms around me. He rests his forehead against mine.

"I missed this," he whispers.

"Me too."

"I love you, Megan. Please give me another chance to show you how good we can be together. My soul is bound to you, and I'm not me without you."

I bring a hand up to his face. Knowing I need to open up to him now; I don't think I can stand another night in an empty bed.

"Breaking up with you was the stupidest thing I've ever done. I thought I was protecting you and your family. Instead, it did exactly what I was trying to stop from happening. I hate sleeping in an empty bed. I miss being in your arms. I love you, Hunter, and if you'll give me another chance, I promise to get the full story from now on. It will be you and me against the world, and the next time we fight, I'll serve you TV dinners instead of walking away."

"It was never a question if I'd give you a second chance; it's always been when you were ready to want it," he whispers then leans in slowly, giving me time to stop or pull away. I close the gap, and my lips land on his.

The kiss is full of need and passion. It's full of I'm sorry, and I need you. He wraps his hand around the back of my neck and pulls me in closer. I gasp. He uses the opportunity to slide his tongue into my mouth and deepen the kiss while keeping it achingly slow.

He pulls away and kisses down my neck as his hand comes to my waist and slips under my shirt. He rubs the skin there for just a few passes then slides his hand up my rib cage. He moves slowly but firmly then pushes my bra out of the way and grabs a handful on my breast, and we both groan.

He pinches my hard nipples and then slides over to my other breast, shoving my bra up and out of the way before massaging it. He trails kisses back up my neck and finds my mouth again as he massages my breasts. I tangle my hands in his hair, pulling him closer to me.

He breaks the kiss, grabs my waist, and lifts me onto his desk.

"I always had a fantasy about taking you here in my office on my desk," he whispers in my ear before biting my ear lobe.

"Show me," I say and pull my shirt off, followed by my bra. Hunter groans and his eyes are glued to my chest.

"You're sealing your fate if you go any further, Megan. You'll never be able to get rid of me."

"I don't want to ever get rid of you. I want to feel you so deep, I feel you for days."

"God, I love you." He pulls his shirt off.

He places a hand on my shoulder and pushes me down until I'm lying on his desk. Then he unbuttons my jeans, slides them and my panties off, and spreads my legs. He runs his hands up the inside of my thighs until he reaches my center. He swipes a finger down my slit.

"You're so wet, baby."

"It was watching you work before I came in here that did it. You aren't the only one with fantasy involving this desk."

He groans and falls to his knees, pulling my ass to the edge of the desk. I feel his tongue licking me and then sucking hard on my clit.

"Hunter!" I scream as my hips buck. He puts one hand on my lower belly to hold me in place and brings the other hand up to thrust a finger into me.

I'm already on edge, I know it won't take long. I feel my orgasm crushing me and when he hooks his finger inside me, it crashes into me. My thighs lock around his head, and I scream his name as wave after wave of pleasure crash into me.

"Another," he growls before he's right back at it, forcing two more orgasms from me before standing up and pulling down his pants and boxer briefs. He reaches up and cups my breasts, one in each hand then slides his hands slowly down my rib cage to my thighs and pulls them apart.

He leans down and kisses me. "I love you, Megan."

"I love you too, Hunter," I moan as I feel the head of his cock at my entrance. He takes one of my nipples into his mouth and sucks hard. At the same time, he thrusts hard all the way into me, causing me to scream his name and arch my back off the desk.

He lightly bites my nipple before placing his hands on my waist and thrusts into me.

"Harder, Hunter. I won't break."

"Fuck."

He thrusts harder, hitting a spot inside me that sends electric sparks down all the nerves in my body. I feel so full, and everything seems right for the first time in weeks. I'm trying to find something to grip onto when I reach the edge of his desk.

I meet his thrusts and feel his fingers digging into my hips before one hand trails to my clit and rubs it hard.

"Come for me, Megan. I'm so close."

Still circling my clit, he leans in and bites one of my nipples, and the pain mixed with the pleasure of him inside me causes me to come again. A few more strokes and he follows me right over the edge. He falls forward, and his head lands on my chest, but he doesn't pull out.

He places a kiss on the center of my chest, right in the valley of my breasts, then reaches for the tissues on his desk to clean himself and me before helping me get dressed again.

"I don't think I can move now," I say as I sit in his chair and watch him get dressed. He laughs, the first time I've heard him laugh in over a week.

He picks me up. "Come on, let's check in the shop, then we have to see Mom."

It's a short drive down to the shop. When we walk in hand in hand, everyone cheers.

"Everything good with team Megtur?" Jill asks.

"No, it's team Huntgan," Anna Mae says.

"Guys, no cutesy names, but yes, everything is good. Thank you for lunch today." Anna Mae waves her hand at me.

The little old ladies all take turns hugging Hunter and asking how his mom is and if he needs anything. When they find out that's our next stop, they all want him to say hi to them.

After a quick stop at his parents' home to pack a bag of their stuff, we're on our way to see his mom, hand in hand.

Chapter 23

Hunter

Mom has spent five days in the hospital, and Dad has just taken her home today. She's demanding a family dinner tonight. Sage and Riley, along with Megan's mom Helen have spent all day cooking casseroles and other foods to fill the freezer for Dad to just heat up, but I don't think they're the only ones.

The ladies of Rock Springs will start showing up tomorrow with food, wanting to check in on Mom, and they'll time it out, so they have food every night for a week or two. I'm sure there's some super-secret signup sheet we don't know about; it happens every time a family in town is in need.

The clinic is doing well. I've canceled the house calls but keep the clinic appointments so there isn't a huge backlog for Dad when he gets back to work. Everyone has been so understanding.

The best part of the past five days has been Megan. She's mine again and being able to hold her and fall asleep with her in my arms again has been heaven. This time I plan to tie her down for good before she has any more silly ideas of trying to get away from me.

I'm on my way to my parents' house. Megan has been there for a few hours, having taken over the food. They all think I had a house call that I couldn't postpone, but I went to talk to Megan's dad and her family.

Her mom cried, and her dad approved. Sage punched me in the arm, saying it was about fucking time. The guys all clapped me on the back and said I was already family. So now it's all about timing. She deserves the killer proposal that's just over the top, and I plan to give it to her.

I pull into the driveway and hop out, heading into the house. Mom is in the living room with her feet propped up, resting like the doctor said but still yelling across the house.

"Now you put those vegetables on the sheet pan. The long one, not the short one with the tall sides."

"Yes, Donna, I know which one you use," Megan calls back.

Mom turns to me with a big smile. "Hey baby, how's the clinic?"

"Good. Everyone is understanding, so it's not too bad," I say and lean over to give her a kiss. "How are you doing?"

"Oh, I'm fine. I don't know why the doctor won't let me at least up and cooking in my own kitchen."

I just laugh. "I'll check on them. Make sure they're using the right sheet pan."

"Yes, the long one with short sides!"

I smile and head into the kitchen to find Megan and Dad.

"Hey baby," I say and kiss Megan on the cheek. "Hey, Dad." I pat him on the back. "What can I do to help?"

"Oh, we got this. We put in Mom's lasagna, but your mom decided she wanted some veggies too and some bread, so we have that going, using the correct sheet pan, as you can see." Megan does her little model pose, holding her hands over the sheet pan.

"Good, you don't need the wrath of Momma. How was your day at the shop?"

"Oh, I only had a half day today, and it was good. More people were in to ask about your mom than anything else."

I chuckle. "Well, I'm going to keep her company, if you two have this covered."

"Yes, go stop her from hollering in here at us," Dad says.

I head back to the living room.

"They're using the right sheet pan. I saw it with my own two eyes," I say and sit in the chair across from her.

"Good. Good. How are you and Megan doing, sweetheart?"

I smile, and that says all it needs to with Mom. "We're doing great actually."

"I don't think I've fully forgiven your father, but this will be his first proper meal since that day at the clinic."

"Mom, he's been eating hospital food. I think that punishment enough."

She grunts but smiles at me.

"In fact, I think you were so mad at him, you planned this car accident to force him to eat hospital food, and force Megan and I back together. You can't convince me otherwise."

I know that's not true, but if Mom could have orchestrated something on this level, she sure as hell would have and even taken the credit for doing so.

"Hunter! How dare you say that. I would never! This was all the good man upstairs stepping in and telling all you Norwood men you're idiots."

I laugh. "Mama, I don't think God would tell us we're idiots."

"No, but I would."

Megan and Dad come into the living room then and as Megan goes to walk past me, I grab her wrist and pull her into my lap. Mom and Dad both smile; they acted just like this as I was growing up.

"Dinner should be ready in about fifteen minutes," Dad says.

"Good, good. Megan, how's the shop going? And that new girl?" Mom asks.

"Anna Mae, she's doing well. People are starting to trust her, so her schedule is booking up, which is relieving some of our schedules. She's taking walk-ins and doing nails. She fits right in, and the girls love her. She worked at a salon in Dallas, so she has some city ideas we must tone down a bit, but she's getting the hang of it. She did mention some hair show or convention in Dallas where you go and show off what you can do. I have no interest in it, but I think it would be good to get the shop's name out there. I think she and Jill are going to go."

"Well, I've never heard of such a thing," Mom says.

"That makes two of us." Megan laughs.

They go on talking about what Anna Mae has told her about the show and when it is, but all I can think about is her sitting on my lap. My hand on her waist rubs circles on her skin, and my other hand is on her upper thigh which is exposed thanks to the cut-off shorts she's wearing.

Since getting back together, we haven't been separated much, other than work. When she's near, I can't seem to keep my hands off her. Something about needing to know she's there and us getting back together wasn't a dream. She's taken it in stride too and now laughs when I make a big show of getting my hands on her.

A timer goes off, and she hops up, causing me to growl.

"I have to check on dinner," she says and then leans over to give me a kiss.

I watch her go then turn back to my parents both, who have smiles on their faces.

Then Mom whispers, "So, when are you going to ask her?"

"I don't know what you're talking about," I say but of course I do. She wants to know when I'm going to ask Megan to marry me, but I'm not talking about this here on the off chance she hears anything. So, I stand.

"I'm going to see if Megan needs any help," I say and head toward the kitchen.

I hear Mom giving me her famous, "Mmm-Hmmm." It's her way of saying she knows the truth, but she'll let it slide for now.

I walk into the kitchen. "Hey baby, what can I do to help?"

"Well, you can set the table. I'm just finishing getting this salad together, and everything is done."

Over dinner, I can't seem to keep my hands off Megan, even though she's sitting right beside me. I have my hand on her thigh, or my arms over her chair, and my fingers on her shoulder or neck. Other times, I'm just holding her hand.

Dad is doing the same thing to Mom, and I notice it doesn't escape their attention either. We talk about the clinic, and I get Dad caught up on what's going on. He plans to stop in for a half-day tomorrow since Megan's mom is coming over to spend some time with Mom, that way she isn't alone.

I guess the ladies have a schedule set up, so Dad can do half days for a bit, and they can come to socialize with Mom and not leave her alone. Again, that's Rock Springs for you. I still haven't seen this super-secret signup sheet.

After dinner, Megan and I head home, and the day ends like I hope every day will for the rest of my life. With me inside Megan, followed by her in my arms in my bed. I need to speed up my plans to make sure that happens.

Chapter 24

Megan

With Hunter's dad back at work part-time, he's been doing house calls again. I guess he's been running around all day because he missed our lunch date but did have Jo deliver food for me. Everyone has been stopping in to see his dad at the clinic or taking turns swinging by to spend time with his mom, so she isn't alone while his dad is at work.

While I take time to help reschedule appointments at the clinic and be there for Hunter and his dad, people finally warm up to Anna Mae, and she now has a steady stream of appointments. It has allowed me to work my chair part-time and concentrate on the business end of the shop.

I've looked into this hair show Anna Mae has talked about, and I think it will be good for her and Jill to do and get our name out there. I don't think people will make the long drive out here from Dallas, but it will draw some attention with neighboring towns.

Anna Mae has fit right in at the shop and in the town. I've asked her if she has thought about staying, but she isn't sure. Her husband isn't fighting too hard on the divorce; since his secretary wound up pregnant, there's no denying the cheating now. Another few months, and she'll be done with him. She hasn't opened up about any of her plans.

When I get home to the ranch, I see Hunter beat me home. I head in but only find Riley in the kitchen.

"Hey, where's Hunter?" I ask her.

"Oh, Sage has him checking on a few cows in the pasture right here. They should be back any time."

I get to set the table and a few minutes later, Sage and Hunter walk in.

"Hey, baby." Hunter kisses me and takes my hand. "Let's go for a walk."

"Dinner will be ready in just a few minutes," I say, confused.

"We have a date tonight." He pulls me out the door.

Hand in hand, we walk through the pasture toward our meadow where we pick wildflowers in the spring.

"Last time I took a walk this way, I found that cow in labor."

"It was the day that started all this. You and me and that kiss. Damn, Megan, that kiss was hot as hell. I think about it every time I walk into the barn. It's very awkward getting hard walking into the barn with your brothers around." He laughs.

"Can't say I'm sorry about that." I laugh.

He smiles. "I'm not either."

The sun is almost set, so Hunter turns the light on his phone as we cross through the trees to get to the clearing. I'm so concentrated on looking down at where I'm stepping, I don't see the clearing right away.

When I look up, what I see takes my breath away. Along a section of trees on the side of the clearing, there are mason jars strung along the trees with candles inside, giving the whole area a mystical fairy light feeling. There's a makeshift wood dance floor in front of the trees surrounded by rose petals. On the dance floor, the petals form a large heart.

"What did you do?" I ask in wonder as I stare at it. He takes my hand, and we walk to the middle of the dance floor, in the middle of the heart of rose petals. He pulls out his phone and a minute later, slow music starts playing.

"Dance with me?" he asks.

"Of course, I love dancing with you."

He pulls me into his arms, and we dance through a few slow songs that seem to describe our relationship and how we feel about each other. Hunter sings each one to me as we dance. After the third song is over, he pulls back and looks into my eyes.

"Dad always said to put my money where my mouth is. Words are just words unless backed up with action. I watched him my whole life, showing Mom how he felt about her with little things. He always made time for her no matter if it was a night like this or just spending time cooking dinner together."

He smiles and gives me a chaste kiss. "So here I am, putting my money where my mouth is. We're amazing together, Megan. When I'm with you, I feel whole. When we're apart, I feel like a part of me is missing. I love knowing I'm coming home to you, good or bad I don't care. I just care that you're there."

He smiles then drops down on one knee. Knowing what's coming, my eyes water. "I'll spend the rest of my life showing you how amazing we are together because there is no one I'd rather marry than my best friend. Megan, will you be my wife?"

I'm so choked up I can't talk at first, so I just nod before croaking out, "Yes!"

The smile that crosses Hunter's face is blinding, and he slips the perfect princess-cut ring on my finger and swoops me up into his arms for a panty-dropping kiss.

He pulls me over to a blanket laid on the ground with a picnic.

"I think I promised you dinner."

We sit and plan the wedding and the future we've always wanted. Knowing I'll get to spend the rest of my life with my best friend is a feeling beyond words.

Epilogue

Megan

A Few Weeks Later

Today Sage and Colt are getting married. We girls are all piled into Sage's room, since it's the best bedroom at the house. It's a tradition we started when Riley got married a few months ago. I, of course, am doing everyone's hair and makeup.

Since Sage isn't getting married until late afternoon, and we started early, I've been able to take my time. It helps that she wants everyone to have a natural look. Her bridesmaid dresses are this beautiful dark-blue teal with a high hem in the front and a low hem in the back.

She's having us wear our cowboy boots with them, so it still has a very country wedding ambiance. Her dress has a beautiful vintage feel to it with lots of lace and only a six-inch train. There's no tulle or extra poof to the dress and when we all see her in the dress, we know it's just very Sage.

The guys have been off doing their thing all day, and we still have an hour before the ceremony. I'm starting to miss Hunter. He was up and out of bed before I was today. We didn't get much sleep last night, as we had been lying in bed planning our wedding.

We decided that he'll move into my room at the ranch and stay here at least until we have kids. Then we'd revisit it like Blaze and Riley planned to do. Hunter did make a few changes to my room, adding some family photos and his own desk, so he can pull records as needed at home.

As for our wedding? We still have a few months, but it will also be at the ranch church. Pastor Greg is over the moon excited to do another wedding at the church here at the ranch.

I get pulled from my thoughts with a knock on the door, and Hunter peeks his head in.

"Can I steal my fiancée for a few minutes?" he asks, and everyone laughs. He has been calling me his fiancée any chance he gets, and I love hearing it.

When I follow him out to the hallway, he pulls me into our room and pushes me up against the door.

"I'm sorry you're going to have to redo your makeup, but I missed you too damn much," he says as his lips land on mine. I dig my nails into his hair and pull him closer.

"I can't wait to rip this dress off you tonight. The last wedding we went to, you weren't mine yet, but this time I get to sleep with the bridesmaid, and it's so damn hot."

"Well," I say laughing, "I get to sleep with one of the groomsmen, so score to me."

"As long as that groomsman is me, you can sleep with him as much as you want tonight."

"I think you have a good chance seeing as how the other groomsmen are my brothers," I say scrunching up my nose, causing him to laugh.

"Get your sexy ass back in that room, and I'll see you at the church," he says, giving me one more kiss and sending me back to Sage's room.

I touch up my makeup, and we do a bridesmaid toast of whiskey. Because we are cowgirls and don't toast with that champagne them city girls drink. Sage's words, not mine.

Riley does a shot of apple juice, being pregnant and all.

We make our way to the church and once we make sure Colt is already inside, we head down the aisle in pairs. Hunter and I are the third pair to go in. My arm in his, and his hand on mine, we make the slow walk to the front of the church.

"Soon, it will be our turn, and I'll be up there watching you walk down the aisle," he whispers to me.

I smile back at him. "I can't wait."

Sage has planned things differently since her best friends are the guys who are Colt's best friends too, and my brothers. She didn't want to do the traditional guys on one side and girls on the other, so we get to stand in pairs scattered across the stage. This allows Hunter and me to stand together arm in arm for the whole wedding.

Watching Sage and Colt today is bittersweet. It means things in the family structure are changing again, but it also is amazing to watch them pledge themselves to each other after all the ups and downs they had and the years apart.

After the wedding and the pictures, we all head to the event barn for Sage's reception.

She had decorated the barn, giving it a very rustic feel. Lots of burlap and lace everywhere, paired with wood and mason jars.

Hunter and I spend a lot of time on the dance floor, but on one slow song, his dad asks to cut in.

"Take care of her, Dad. I'm going to find Mom and drag her out for a dance."

He goes off, and Hank takes me for a spin on the dance floor.

"I want to apologize again for my role in splitting you two up. And I wanted to say how proud I am of you two being able to work through it. It's how I know you'll have an amazing marriage."

"What do you mean?"

"Marriage isn't all sunshine and roses, as my wife says. We fight and have disagreements, but we don't walk away. We work them out. Sometimes right then and there, sometimes a few hours later, and sometimes a few days later. To have a good marriage, you have to have the skills to forgive and work the problem out."

"Mom and Dad say the same thing. We kids have seen them fight. They've never hidden it from us, but they also always work it out, so I learned that from a young age."

"That's good. It's a skill that's hard to teach as you get older and more set in your ways."

I laugh. The song wraps up, and Hunter's right there, handing his mom back into his dad's arms and taking me back in his.

After a few more dances, I have to sit and give my feet a rest. Hunter goes to get us some drinks, and I people watch.

Blaze and Riley are all cozied up at their table, talking and laughing. I'm sure they're remembering their wedding just a short time ago.

Sage and Colt are still out on the dance floor. They've always loved to dance together as much as Hunter and I do. Hunter's parents are still on the dance floor, and my parents are off to the side talking to some of their friends.

It takes me a minute to spot Mac off in one of the corners, his nose in his phone. I'm thinking he's met someone, but he won't talk about it.

The only person I don't see is Jason. Hunter comes back with some water for both of us.

"Have you seen Jason?" I ask him.

"Oh yeah, he's over there." He points to a table towards the back of the barn.

Sure enough, there he is talking to a blond girl I've never seen before, and it looks like her parents are at the table too. There are quite a few people here I've never seen before. After high school, Sage took off and traveled for a few years and made lots of friends along the way.

I keep an eye on Jason, and he's completely taken by this girl who looks even younger than I am. Interesting. Then she smiles at him, and he gets the same glazed look in his eyes that Hunter gets when he looks at me right before he says he loves me.

Yep, my big brother is a goner, and I don't even know who the girl is.

Hunter leans over. "Ready to get out of here? I want to peel that dress off you and act out my sleeping with the bridesmaid fantasy."

"Mmm, I can be persuaded to leave and go home."

Hunter has me out of the barn and heading home so fast it makes my head spin. When we finally fall into bed later that night, I can't wipe the smile off my face. Life with my best friend who knows me better than I know myself has its perks.

The kind that comes with orgasms.

• • • ● • ● • • • •

Want more Megan and Hunter? **Join my mailing list to get a bonus epilogue!**

https://www.kacirose.com/ObsessionBonus

Make sure to get Jason and Ella's story next
in **The Cowboy and His Sweetheart.**

More Books by Kaci M. Rose

Rock Springs Texas Series
The Cowboy and His Runaway – Blaze and Riley
The Cowboy and His Best Friend – Sage and Colt
The Cowboy and His Obsession – Megan and Hunter
The Cowboy and His Sweetheart – Jason and Ella
The Cowboy and His Secret – Mac and Sarah
Rock Springs Weddings Novella
Rock Springs Box Set 1-5 + Bonus Content

Cowboys of Rock Springs
The Cowboy and His Mistletoe Kiss – Lilly and Mike
The Cowboy and His Valentine – Maggie and Nick

The Cowboy and His Vegas Wedding –
Royce and Anna
The Cowboy and His Angel – Abby and
Greg
The Cowboy and His Christmas Rockstar –
Savannah and Ford
The Cowboy and His Billionaire – Brice and
Kayla

Connect with Kaci M. Rose

Kaci M. Rose writes steamy small town cowboys. She also writes under Kaci Rose and there she writes wounded military heroes, giant mountain men, sexy rock stars, and even more there. Connect with her below!

Website
Facebook
Kaci Rose Reader's Facebook Group
Goodreads
Book Bub
Join Kaci M. Rose's VIP List (Newsletter)

About Kaci M Rose

Kaci M Rose writes cowboy, hot and steamy cowboys set in all town anywhere you can find a cowboy.

She enjoys horseback riding and attending a rodeo where is always looking for inspiration.

Kaci grew on a small farm/ranch in Florida where they raised cattle and an orange grove. She learned to ride a four-wheeler instead of a bike (and to this day still can't ride a bike) and was driving a tractor before she could drive a car.

Kaci prefers the country to the city to this day and is working to buy her own slice of land in the next year or two!
Kaci M Rose is the Cowboy Romance alter ego of Author Kaci Rose.

See all of Kaci Rose's Books here.

Please Leave a Review!

I love to hear from my readers! Please **head over to your favorite store and leave a review** of what you thought of this book!

Made in the USA
Columbia, SC
14 May 2024